BARRINGER HOUSE

BARRINGER HOUSE

Barbara Riefe

Five Star

Five Star Romance
Published in conjunction with
Sharon Jarvis & Co., Literary Agency.

Cover photograph by Holly Lidstone

February 2000

Five Star Standard Print Romance Series.

The text of this edition is unabridged.

Set in 11 pt. Plantin by Minnie B. Raven.

Printed in the United States on permanent paper.

Library of Congress Cataloging-in-Publication Data

Riefe, Barbara, 1925–
Barringer House / by Barbara Riefe.
p. cm.
ISBN 0-7862-2337-5 (hc : alk. paper)
1. Young women — New England — Fiction. I. Title.
PS3568.I3633 B37 2000
813′.54—dc21 99-054985

BARRINGER HOUSE

1

The day coach swayed gently, groaning and whining like a living creature as the train hurtled northward through the dismal October gloom. Night was coming on, stealing over the land like a coverlet drawn slowly over a sleeping child to ward off the chill. The insistent clacking of the rails beneath the floorboards of the coach dulled Alison's senses and she shifted her weight in an attempt to find a more comfortable position. But the slatted, high-backed seat allowed for none. Sighing disconsolately, she turned her head to glance out the window at the darkening landscape rushing by.

Early in the month though it was, the trees—rock maples and hickories, oaks and paper birches—were already adorning themselves with the bright hues of autumn, the leaves displaying butter yellows, leathery maroons, and the rock maples showing an opulence of orange, each single leaf a tiny fire contributing to a huge conflagration engulfing one tree after another.

But even this colorful relief in the otherwise gloomy landscape did little to elevate Alison's spirits. It was not alone her mission that depressed her, the fact that the baggage car two cars behind her contained, among its mail sacks and crates of various sizes and dimensions, a single oaken casket solely in her charge; it was the annoying and bitter memory of that evening two weeks earlier. And Adrian Peale.

Dear Adrian, with his wavy blond hair, blue eyes and glib manner. Dear handsome Adrian, whom every woman adored and every man viewed with mingled envy and admiration. To think that the two of them had actually been engaged, until that fateful moment when like Jericho's walls, the whole affair came tumbling down.

On that blackest of all black days she had left the school shortly before the noon hour, intending to shop in Altmeyer Street, then run to Spauldings for a quick bite before returning to work. But try as she might, she was unable to find anything to please her in the shops. The dresses she did examine were either outrageously expensive or depressingly homely. And so her mood was nothing to envy when fifteen minutes after the time she had allotted herself for shopping she hurried into Spauldings, and turning a corner guarded by a dusty potted palm was greeted by the sight of Adrian sitting at a table for two with Emily Charters.

It wasn't merely that she came upon him holding Emily's hand and leaning too obviously close to her in order to whisper something, it was the expression on his handsome face as he recognized her. Guilt was never so cleverly captured on any artist's canvas. It was as if a mask displaying instantaneous contrition had suddenly materialized to cover his face, his eyes growing enormous, his jaw dropping and the color draining from his cheeks with the rapidity of a filled pail overturning.

From the moment she had accepted Adrian's ring in exchange for her promise of marriage, she had heard rumors. But she had discounted them, attributing every vicious word to jealousy on the part of the tale bearer. Over and over again she assured herself that Adrian was faithful, his every word truthful, and that he would never hurt her. Not for the world.

And all the time, all the days of all the long happy weeks, he had been laughing at her, playing her for the fool, using her to bolster his ego, elevating her to a pedestal in the gallery of his conquests. And Emily Charters' silly laugh was merely the final twist to the knife in the wound.

That night she had confronted him and they had had it out, a loud, decidedly unpleasant but necessary row, name calling and accusations—of jealousy and childishness on her part and lying, deceit and outright callousness on his. She had capped the incident by flinging his ring at him and stalking out of his rooms, slamming the door on what had to be the most humiliating single episode of her life. It wasn't what he had done to her that angered her, nor even Emily Charters' laughter—first voice in what was doubtless to become a chorus of the same from one end of Philadelphia to the other. It was her own stupidity, her blind loyalty, her faithfulness lavished full measure on a man who had never loved her from the first moment they'd met.

It was dark now, pitch black outside, the sky and the earth joining in a single solid shadow torn here and there by the lighted windows of the farmhouses racing by. She studied her face in the mist-stained window. It was a good face, not beautiful perhaps, not blessed with the lofty cheekbones, the flawless skin, the lovely eyes and hair that Emily Charters so haughtily displayed, but a face that sparkled with life and warmth. My pretty Princess Peachblossom her father had called her.

She glanced at the palm of her left hand and her finger where the outline of Adrian's ring betrayed itself across the soft pink flesh. Adrian. She could only hope that one day an Emily Charters or someone as beautiful, as greedy and demanding would accord him the same treatment. Certain she was that no man breathing deserved it more.

The three yellow lamps spaced ten feet apart along the ridge of the ceiling of the coach joined their feeble glow, barely permitting her to distinguish the heads of the three other occupants seated in front of her. The conductor appeared in the doorway at the opposite end. He came forward, pulling his way seat by seat, pausing as he reached her, touching the brim of his cap courteously and smiling.

"If you find it a bit chilly, miss, you might like to move forward one car. There's a stove there."

"Thank you. I'm not at all cold."

"Getting off at Brunswick, aren't you?" Alison nodded as he took out his watch and studied it. "Hour and twenty minutes."

Again he smiled, touched his cap and walked off. She thrust her hand into her reticule and brought out a magazine, the new monthly *Harper's.* It was March, 1851, the first issue. The fiction was marvelous, she had already managed three of the stories between New York and Boston when the coaches were crowded with passengers and an elderly man smelling of stale whiskey had sat beside her, alternately chewing his mustache and drumming on his knees with his fingertips. Now, thanks to the brothers Harper, she would lose herself in a certain Mr. Tait's explorations in the Nile delta, where no one remotely resembling either Adrian Peale or Emily Charters was to be found.

But the light was too dim and she was too tired to read, certainly to enjoy what she was reading. It had been a tiresome week. On the heels of Adrian's defection, rather his expulsion, and the untimely death of her father, the long train trip was also taking something out of her. She had three of Dr. Monroe's loathsome iron pills left in the small pink box in her bag, and securing the box and the handleless tin cup she always carried with her when traveling, she arose from her seat and moved forward toward the drinking water tank at the far end of the coach.

The iron pill went down hard and as bitter as gall and in the next ten minutes did nothing whatsoever to restore her waning energy. Earlier she had tried to nap, but the shrill clatter and squeaking of the train made it impossible and instead she had passed the time between New York and Boston in her magazine.

She glanced at her watch suspended from the slender silver chain around her neck. Forty-three minutes to Brunswick. Cousin Charles would be waiting for her. She had not met Charles since the two of them were children, that is since she was six or seven, he being at least eight years older. He had to be twenty-nine or thirty now, a full-fledged surgeon on the staff of the East Cumberland County Hospital in some place called Harwich, according to her mother. Alison pictured him as a gangling fifteen-year-old. He had had, she recalled, the most peculiar laugh, a spontaneous cackle better suited to an old witch than a growing boy. But he was well mannered, and his company enjoyable.

There was little else she could remember about Cousin Charles Collier, except that he was her father's sister Kate's second son. Alison had been assured by daddy's lawyer before departing from home that Charles would be taking care of everything in Wiscasset, including arranging for a place for her to stay. It had been her father's dying wish that he be returned to the town where he'd been born and brought up, to be interred in the family plot. It was, she reflected, charitable of Cousin Charles to take the time and trouble to fulfill the last wish of an uncle he had neither seen nor heard from in fifteen years.

Cousin Charles. He would be tall and probably good looking and perhaps his laugh had lowered in pitch to a level more befitting his station in life.

She closed her eyes and saw the casket packed in the corner of the baggage car. It was not a particularly impressive journey home for such a fine man, one taken from life before his fifty-first year. Alison's mother had been unable to accompany her, being laid up in bed mending a broken hip suffered in a fall downstairs. She had not wanted to leave her mother to the care of Lydia, the maid, but her mother had insisted that Alison go to Maine. And so here she was.

Oddly, unexpectedly, Adrian had come down to the Broad Street station to see her off, an act of penance she imagined. At that, it was practically the first display of genuine concern for the feelings of another she could credit him with. Whatever his motive and despite his profuse apologies, his surprise appearance changed nothing between them. The abyss had been cut, wide and deep, and there would be no bridging it. If she was to be ridiculed because she had associated herself with a man who held her in such obvious low esteem, breaking with him only to resume the alliance at a later date begged more than ridicule, more than scorn.

So much for Adrian Peale.

Rounding a seemingly endless curve, the train slowed and the lamps of the Brunswick station pierced the gloom. Again she consulted her watch. It was nearly a quarter to eight. The station drew closer and presently the train stopped alongside the platform with a violent jolt, all but hurling her against the back of the unoccupied seat in front of her. Getting up, she gripped her reticule and her mother's valise and made her way down the aisle to the far end where her friend the conductor helped her down the steps.

"They're taking the casket off here, you know," she said, a trace of concern in her tone.

He leaned out, looking down the length of the train. "It's coming off now. The station agent will have your bill of lading."

"Goodbye and thank you."

"You're going back?"

"Day after tomorrow."

"Perhaps we shall meet again."

"I hope so."

She stood on the platform and watched the train pull out of the station, down the plumb-straight run of tracks. The twin red lamps at the rear of the last car glared like the eyes of some creature of fantasy gradually shrinking and vanishing from sight.

The platform was deserted. The trainmen, having unloaded the casket, had left it on a baggage truck. Turning, she made her way toward it, her heels clicking hollowly. A fine gray mist had settled over the station, blending the hazy white lamps into a single dull glow. The familiar odor of burning coal touched her nostrils and a man in shirt, vest and rumpled trousers appeared in the doorway waving a piece of pink paper.

"You for that casket, miss?"

"Yes."

"Here be your bill of lading." He handed the paper to her and tugged at the left end of his mustache, eyeing her curiously. "Waiting for somebody?"

"My cousin. He was supposed to meet me."

"Where 'bouts he coming from?"

"The hospital."

"He probably be by shortly. Come along inside, why don't you, and set by the stove. There's a nip in the air tonight." He paused and surveyed the sky. "Smells like rain."

He carried her bags inside, setting them on the long bench against the far wall. To her right, as she sat down wearily opposite the open door, a small office presented itself, fronted by the ticket window and a swinging half door that led into an area dominated by a large flat-topped desk stacked with wire baskets filled with papers. The walls were a bilious green and the ceiling yellow with age, cracked and peeling. The two oil lamps standing on the desk amongst the basketed papers threw shadows upward against the ceiling and the smoke rising from the hole in the pipe of the stove in the center of the room settled against it, shrouding it and gathering the shadows to it. In the distance a train hooted, mournfully announcing its imminent arrival to the night.

"That be the ten o'clock for Waterville," said the man, yawning and quickly covering his mouth with his fist.

At that moment there was the sound of hooves and wheels turning followed by a door slamming, and in seconds two men appeared in the doorway.

"Alison?"

Cousin Charles came forward, reaching out for her hand. She recognized him at once although he was considerably bigger and heavier than she had imagined he would be, six feet three or four at least, broad-shouldered and powerful looking. Her hand disappeared as he covered it with his own.

"Charles."

"I'm sorry we're late. Last minute fuss at the hospital held us up. Patients really are the most inconsiderate people. Oh, I beg your pardon. Let me introduce my associate, Mr. Hampton. Gene, my cousin Alison, all the way from Philadelphia. Isn't she a beauty, though?"

Gene Hampton reacted in embarrassment for her and shook her hand.

"Pleasure, Miss Collier."

"Well, let's not stand around this drafty old barn," snapped Charles. "Cousin dear, your carriage awaits. We're taking you to the Speedwell, about twelve miles down the road. Sorry it's so far, but it's the finest spot around this God-forsaken place. You look exhausted and you're probably famished to boot. I'll give Mrs. Tyler, the lady in charge, strict orders to feed you and bed you down post haste."

"The casket . . ."

"A wagon's coming for it. I've arranged for it to be taken directly to Mueller's Funeral Home in Harwich. Don't worry about it. The driver's one of our people from the hospital."

Gene Hampton smiled. "Matter of fact, he's my uncle."

Charles' face darkened. "I am sorry, Alison, about your father I mean. What happened exactly?"

"It started with a chill. He came home from the bank one day in a heavy downpour and with no umbrella. Mother and I both thought it was nothing more than a cold coming on, but by the next morning he was so ill he couldn't get out of bed."

"You called the doctor?"

"At once."

She continued to explain as they made their way to the coach and Charles helped her in, instructing the driver to take them to Harwich and from there to the Speedwell Inn. Settling in, he drew a bearskin robe over her lap. The coach sprang forward, the wheels grinding over the rutted road, the horses' hooves clattering as if striking solid stone, their rhythm punctuated now and again by the driver's shrill cry and the snap of his whip.

"Strangely enough, on the fifth or sixth day daddy began to rally. His fever came down and he got some color back in his cheeks."

"That's generally the way of it," observed Charles. "It's almost as if all the resources of strength and will to live muster for one final onslaught against the inevitable. They try, they fail . . ." He shrugged.

"He died within forty-eight hours."

"A pity, so young."

"Not yet fifty-one."

The conversation turned away from Alison's unhappy mission to Gene Hampton who, it developed, was the assistant administrator at the hospital and in fact had been responsible for engaging Charles two years earlier. The two were obviously close friends. Sitting beside Charles and across from Gene Hampton, she studied him from the concealment of her veil. He did not have Charles' ease of manner, nor his good looks or commanding appearance, but there was something distinctly likeable about the man. His smile, his enthusiasm and a frank desire to please added to the impression. His hair was blazing red, nearly the color of the rock maple leaves burning the trees on the way from Portland to Brunswick; and his complexion was as ruddy as might be expected. It was, however, his eyes that attracted her notice, the manner in which they crinkled at the edges when he brightened and what they said to her when he fixed them upon her: I like you. I would like to know you better. Is it possible?

Preoccupied with the conversation as she was, she scarcely noticed the coach entering Harwich until the driver pulled up in front of the hospital.

"My stop," said Charles, opening the door and rising. He

eyed Gene Hampton mischievously. "You must understand, Alison, I have a very demanding employer. Duty calls, a fussy beldam with a gall bladder that is taking its revenge on her for a lifetime of imprisonment in what has to be the most cantankerous human being you, Mr. Hampton, have ever let through our doors."

Gene Hampton glanced at Alison. "Pay no attention to him. He carries on like this all the time. He's far from overworked. Actually, we treat him like a king; even mediocre surgeons are hard to come by these days."

"Pistols at dawn, you insulting profligate!" Charles laughed, to Alison's surprise, cackled, not unlike the fifteen-year-old boy she had known in years gone by, and got out of the coach. "Gene will see you to the Speedwell Inn, and introduce you to Mrs. Tyler. Hampton, I do hope you will behave yourself. Remember, this lady is my cousin, not one of those barroom wenches with whom you're so fond of associating."

Grasping the handle, Gene pulled the door shut in his face. The coach continued on to the inn and he occupied most of the time regaling her with his lofty opinion of Dr. Charles Collier.

"Without him, the East Cumberland would be in fairly desperate straits. We seem to have more than our share of poor doctors in this part of the country."

"Have you ever had any desire to practice?"

"Desire? Very much so, but neither the intelligence nor the gift."

"You're much too modest."

The coach jounced over the rough narrow road, the horses snorting at the pale moon which had emerged like a single baleful eye staring down checking on worldly activity. Now and again a farmhouse appeared and vanished, its windows lightless, shades drawn tightly, while the occupants escaped to their dreams. Familiar as she was with the bustle of the city, rural Maine seemed like another world entirely, a far-off planet populated by creatures who looked like Philadelphians but, like the Brunswick station master, mouthed strange accents. People who disdained commerce and industry in favor of wresting their livelihood from the land and the sea nearby. To think that her father had been born and raised in such a place. To think that he would want to return to it. But then, why shouldn't he? He had always spoken in glowing terms, with undisguised nostalgia in his voice, of Wiscasset and Maine, of the admirable artlessness and candor of the people, their generosity, their hardiness and resourcefulness, of the lifelong friendships one could establish with one's neighbors, of the spacious freedom of land and sea, in marked contrast to what even the most sophisticated and contended city dweller had to admit was the cramped and stifling ambience of the Philadelphias of the world.

Gene Hampton, like daddy, born and raised in Maine, shared his high opinion of the state. The more he talked, the more impressed Alison became with this friend of Cousin Charles. How different he was from Adrian Peale, how authentic by comparison. Yes, the very word, authentic, real, honest and sincere.

"Charles has arranged for Reverend Milner to conduct the services tomorrow."

"Will you be there?"

"I hadn't . . . that is I didn't know your father."

"If you can, I wish you'd come. You and Charles will be the only ones I'll know. It sounds childish, but I'm afraid I'm not at my best in the company of strangers." She avoided his eyes, fixing her glance on the armada of rain clouds sailing southward overhead. "I must confess I feel so far away from life at this moment, far away from everything I've known and loved. Tomorrow won't be easy. I loved my father very much. He was the most charitable man, the most unselfish, the most human human being I have ever known. He spoiled me unmercifully, oh not with material things, but he was so good, so fine I came to believe that every man was like that. I'm sure you've never met anyone quite as naive as I."

"Nonsense, every girl thinks her father the perfect man. Maybe that's why young men have such a difficult time of it. The footsteps they hope to follow in are large and far between."

"Now you're teasing me."

"On the contrary. I'm perfectly serious." He paused. "And if you're sure I won't be intruding I'll come tomorrow."

"Please do."

They arrived at the Speedwell Inn, a rambling pristine white colonial home studded with green shutters and encircled by stately pines and pin oaks. Gene introduced Alison to Mrs. Tyler who in turn introduced her to a bowl of delicious broth and a warmed-over pot roast that chased her hunger and restored her the strength Dr. Monroe's celebrated bitter pill had been unable to. So many long miles from the doctor's watchful eye, she took the liberty of tossing the last two pills out her bedroom window.

Her room was unusually large, tastefully furnished and crowned with oak beams. Centering the wall opposite the door squarely between two windows overlooking the street was an enormous featherbed which proved to be as soft as a cloud when she sat upon it.

She retired early and slept until eight the following

morning, rising to the gentle patter of the rain against the windows. The station master in Brunswick had read the night sky well. And how fitting, she thought. To have the day of daddy's funeral sun-drenched and beautiful would have been so inappropriate. Better the world care and the heavens sorrow.

Reverend Milner was a tall, spare man affecting thick spectacles, white gloves and a limp that he seemed unnecessarily self-conscious of. A boy half his gangling height stood beside him at the head of the grave shielding his bald head with an umbrella, the downpour thudding dully against the cloth. With Charles holding an umbrella over the two of them at her left side and Gene on her right, she stared down at the toes of her shoes and in front of them the edge of the grave, studying the small indentations pocking the dark brown earth, the raindrops striking and running in tiny rivulets down into the hole.

"Judge me, O Lord; for I have walked in mine integrity: I have trusted also in the Lord; therefore I shall not slide.

"Examine me, O Lord, and prove me; try my reins and my heart.

"For thy loving-kindness is before mine eyes: and I have walked in thy truth . . ."

There were only thirteen people at the graveside, including the Reverend Milner and his assistant. The casket was brought forward and lowered and the handful of earth, thoughtfully kept dry in a cloth sack, cast down upon it. Alison stared at the box and, like a wave of nausea, a desperate melancholy took hold of her as the others in attendance turned away from the site and started down the long hill toward their waiting carriages.

At Alison's request there was to be no post-ceremony gathering. Charles had introduced her to everyone prior to their departure from the Speedwell, and as she had told him then she had no wish to make additional demands on the time of those considerate enough to see her father to his eternal rest.

By the time the string of carriages had returned to the inn, the storm had increased in intensity, great sheets of water thrashing down upon the area, the ominous black clouds overhead seemingly bent on punishing the earth beneath for some offense. The water raced down the gutter in front of the inn in torrents and every rut in the road brimmed to overflowing.

Charles and Gene took lunch with her in the dining room where only two other tables were occupied. Understandably, lunch was a solemn occasion characterized throughout by negligible conversation and more nibbling at the Dover sole and fresh garden vegetables than enjoyable eating.

Outside their window, the wind bent the pines toward the house and drove the downpour horizontally against the panes like buckshot from a gun.

The storm sustained its fury throughout the afternoon. The earliest train from Brunswick south to Boston wasn't until nine that evening and both Charles and Gene promised to return at eight to accompany her to the station. She thanked Charles for his many kindnesses and offered to reimburse him for the expenses he had incurred, but he adamantly refused her money.

At seven in the evening, having napped away most of the afternoon in anticipation of her all-night journey home, Alison took her dinner, a broiled lobster and small green salad, in her room. Mrs. Tyler herself brought it upstairs to her. She appeared in the doorway, tray in hand, wearing an anxious look on her birdlike features.

"It's getting awfully mean out there, Miss Collier. Cook tells me she just got word from the grocer that the bridge between here and Harwich has washed away. It's not for me to say, my dear, but if I were you I'd think about staying over one more night. Hopefully this storm will spend itself by morning, but right now it's as fierce as a scalded cat. Every road for miles around is like a river."

"Must I go through Harwich to get to the Brunswick station?"

"No, you can go the shore road, but travel will be no better. It's just no night to be out."

"I appreciate your concern, Mrs. Tyler, and I'd like to stay, but I really must get back to Philadelphia. My mother is indisposed and she expects me. And to be honest, I'm very worried about her, what with the death of my father . . ."

"I think you're making a mistake."

Mrs. Tyler shook her head, but at the same time studied her with admiration in her eyes. "You young girls today are a plucky lot. Very well, if your mind's made up, I'll get Tom Burgess to drive you. He's the best with reins in hand in Cumberland County. And a teetotaler."

"Thank you, but that won't be necessary. Dr. Collier and Mr. Hampton are coming for me at eight."

"Not with the Harwich bridge out they're not." She sighed and pondered a moment. "It's already past seven. Even if they know about the bridge and have already started, they'll likely not be here for an hour and a half what with detouring. You'll never make your train if you wait for them. If you're going, you'd best leave right away. Better to wait at the station than here. Then, too, you'll need the time, in case Tom has to detour off the shore road. I'd best send the boy to fetch him right away."

Alison hesitated. If only there were some way to get word to Charles and Gene. But there was none.

"Maybe you're right. But if the doctor and Mr. Hampton do show up, please explain for me," she said.

"Of course, dear."

Paying her bill and thanking Mrs. Tyler for her hospitality and assistance, Alison was helped into the coach by Tom Burgess, an elderly grizzled man affecting a patch over his left eye. And away they went.

Burgess drove slowly. Allison sat back in the corner of the coach and watched the storm assault the window, the rain whipping against the glass. The coach was large, almost as big as a diligence. The seats were covered with Moroccan leather and so comfortable she wished she might take one with her when she boarded her train. The interior had been carefully cleaned, the walnut paneling highly polished and the linings of brown velvet appeared new. However, a disagreeable odor of tobacco lingered in the air, a reminder that she was not the first to ride with Tom Burgess that day. So strong was the presence of the tobacco that she considered opening the door to let in fresh air, but more rain than air would surely come in if she did so, so she wisely rejected the impulse.

Lightning turned the world outside blue-white and directly overhead thunder crackled like a tree splintering. The coach rumbled along, the horses challenging the storm, Burgess' voice now and again rising above the wind to urge them onward. They had traveled no more than fifteen minutes when lightning glowed and through the window she saw that they were passing the cemetery where her father had been buried earlier in the day. No sooner had the lightning revealed the gate and the small army of headstones ascending the hill than a second bolt defined its summit against the sky. There was no mistaking the single oak tree, bent and disfigured by so many similar storms, but it was not the tree that gripped her eyes and sent a shock wave of horror coursing through her body. It was the scene taking place beside the tree. Two men were clearly visible silhouetted against the white sky, one tall and wearing a stovepipe hat and cloak, the other a head taller, identically garbed against the elements. The second man's back was humped and his head looked as if it were bound to his body not by his neck, but partway down his chest His lower jaw was huge and clearly outlined. The two bore a casket between them, the grisly tableau flashing on, remaining but a split second and vanishing in darkness, its passing punctuated by the rattling roar of thunder.

Alison gripped the door latch and pulling herself to her feet began rapping with her fist against the top of the coach. It lurched forward and she was thrown back onto her seat, but recovering quickly, she wrenched open the door and leaning out braving the downpour, called up to Burgess.

"Did you see that? Did you?"

"See what, mum?" He looked down at her blankly out of his one good eye, twisting his face in a frown.

"Two men, up on that hill. They were carrying a casket . . ."

Burgess shook his head. "Never saw hair of nobody."

"But, I tell you . . . Oh, never mind." She wiped her eyes with the back of her sleeve. "How much further?"

"Six mile. Never fear, we'll make your train, if we move along."

"Yes, yes, move on. I'm sorry . . ."

"It's all right, mum."

She closed the door feeling very wet and very foolish. Of course he hadn't seen anything. How could he, with his one eye on the road and his patched one, his left, on the cemetery side.

Ghouls. Grave robbers, taking advantage of the night and the storm to steal a corpse! If only the bridge outside Harwich hadn't been washed away, if only Charles and Gene had arrived and were with her now. On second thought, perhaps it was just as well they weren't. To stop and investigate would surely cause her to miss her train.

But simple curiosity nagged and tormented her. She must write to Charles as soon as she returned to Philadelphia. He and Gene could investigate the situation, assuming that she was able to convince them that she actually had seen something. Certainly Tom Burgess was no witness. Doubtless as far as he was concerned she had imagined the whole scene.

By now the coach had reached the top of the long hill which had begun just before the main gate to the cemetery. Burgess started his horses down the opposite side, the brake squealing through the sound of wind and rain and the horses clopping along through the quagmire that was the road. All of a sudden she heard Burgess yell and instantly the coach leapt forward gathering speed quickly, lifting her up out of her seat and against the door on the left as the front wheel on that side struck a deep rut and veered dangerously. In the next instant they were out of control and careening dizzily down the hill. Whether the brake had given way, the horses had slipped their traces or Burgess had simply lost control she had no way of knowing, but certain she was that any moment now disaster would be upon them!

Unable to grasp anything, she was flung about the interior, smashing against the door, the seat in front of her and the floor beneath while the coach continued plunging headlong down the hill, faster, faster, faster.

Then it happened. The front wheels struck a stone, a fallen tree or some other obstacle and stopped dead, the rear wheels lifting high in the air, the cumbersome vehicle crashing down on its right side, toppling clear over upside down, its wall panels bursting, the top cracking and splintering like dried twigs. She struck her head against the doorpost, her neck snapping backward, a burning needle of pain lancing through her temple into her brain, and pitch blackness swiftly engulfed her.

The last sounds she heard were the plaintive whinny of one of the horses up the hill behind the wreckage and the rain drumming insistently on a shard of the shattered window pane directly over her head.

2

Crimson clouds billowing round about her . . . thick, seemingly impenetrable, threatening to smother her completely. Around her feet and over her head they swirled, closer and closer as if her body itself was attracting them, drawing them tightly about her, hastening their stifling effect. Instinctively, she reached out to tear them apart, to let in precious air and light.

Red clouds? Even dulled as it was by the numbing pain that enveloped her brain, her sense of awareness failed to accept such a phenomenon. And as her mind rejected the clouds they began to dissolve, to be replaced by flashing lights, a spinning Catherine wheel shooting its colors in every direction.

She tried to open her eyes, to break the grip of the incubus, but failed in the attempt, unable to muster the strength necessary to lift her lids. Then the Catherine wheel vanished as suddenly as it had appeared and darkness settled over her, no swirling clouds now but a black cloak, as solid as a vein of coal. Disembodied eyes, bulging and rheumy, appeared at a distance directly before her. They began moving through the darkness, closer and closer, staring dully as they came, peering through her, larger and larger, great round gaping windows . . .

She tried to scream, but could not utter a sound, succeeding only in flinging a flash of light across her mind that veiled the oncoming eyes for a brief moment before vanishing.

"Otto!"

The voice was miles away, scarcely audible. Her eyes opened to discover the bulging, dull eyes within an inch of her own.

"OTTO!"

The eyes drew back, the man straightening, backing away, his thick lips quivering, his massive head shaking from side to side. A woman stepped in front of him, pushing him back with her left hand. Her face was kindly, her eyes warm and friendly. Over her head as she bent down, Alison saw him retreat to the doorway.

"Leave us!" snapped the woman.

The man turned sideways and for a moment only the upper part of his body was outlined by the lamp in the outside corridor. The great head and lower jaw projecting fully halfway down his chest were unmistakable. The cemetery . . .

She stifled a gasp.

"There, there, my dear, don't be afraid of him. He is harmless. He is a mute . . ."

"Where am I?"

"Safe and sound. Warm and comfy in bed. You were in an accident down the road a piece. Doctor Devereaux and Otto found you."

"The driver . . ."

The friendly face clouded, lips tightening, sadness filling the pale blue eyes. "Dead as a doornail. Broken neck."

"This house . . ."

Her eyes roamed the ceiling and the upper walls, the twin black beams supporting white plaster overhead, capping the dark wainscotting surrounding. To the left, three tall windows outlined the distant moon suspended over a single angry cloud. The rain had stopped, the only evidence of the storm a pattern of dried streaks running vertically down the glass. In the far corner, off the end of the bed in which she lay, stood a small cabriole-table, over it an oval mirror in a gilded wooden frame. But her eyes came back to the center window and the space directly above it. Hanging there was a wooden shield, a curling wave, conches and crossed tridents, evidence of the nearness of the sea and its influence upon this house and, she surmised, those who lived in it.

"Alma."

The woman had been babbling on about nothing of consequence and seemed about to respond to her question when the voice interrupted. Framed in the doorway was a man of medium height, broad-shouldered and thick-necked. No sooner had he spoken than he stepped forward into the candlelight. His face was the color of parchment, his eyes red and malignant, but his voice unusually gentle and he gestured courteously as he came toward the bed.

"Miss . . ."

"Alison Collier."

"I am Dr. Maartens. This is Barringer House, my home. I am sorry to have to welcome you under such uncomfortable circumstances. You have already met Alma, the lady who takes such excellent care of us here. Alma, Nurse Raphael has been asking for you downstairs." This last was a direct order punctuated by the doctor's fixed stare, an order which Alma responded to without hesitation. She left, muttering indistinguishably, her skirts rustling, her heavy step clomping down the hall. Dr. Maartens drew up a chair and sat down. Gently he touched the pulse at Alison's neck, counting the beats to himself.

"How are you feeling?"

"As well as to be expected, I suppose." She tried to rise, but pain seized her right shoulder and she winced.

"Easy . . ."

"My shoulder, is it broken?"

"Fortunately no, but there is a severe bruise and the contusion on your head will need watching."

Grasping her hand, he lifted her fingers to her right temple. Touching it started more pain. But it wasn't this that surprised her, rather it was the icy coldness of his hand enveloping her own.

"You're a very lucky young lady. You could easily have been crushed to death. My associate, Dr. Devereaux, tells me that your coach was little more than a pile of kindling when he and Alma's brother Otto came upon it."

"Alma tells me Mr. Burgess was killed . . ."

"I'm afraid so. There was nothing they could do for him, his neck was broken. John, Dr. Devereaux has taken the body back to Wiscasset. Your coach was coming from that direction."

She explained the reason for her journey to Brunswick, and her concern for her mother.

"My cousin, Dr. Charles Collier, is in residence at the County Hospital. Will it be possible to get word to him and tell him what has happened so that he might contact my mother?"

"Of course. As soon as John gets back I'll send him on to the hospital."

"Do you know Dr. Collier?"

"I'm afraid not. I rarely leave the house, so unfortunately I have little opportunity to meet people."

She studied his eyes. How strange, she thought, there was evil in them all right, as clearly as there was nothing like evil in either his voice or his manner. A strange man this Dr. Maartens, whoever he was.

"It's very late, isn't it?"

He consulted his watch. "After eleven. You were unconscious for more than two hours."

"Charles may not be at the hospital this late. In fact, he may even be out looking for me. He rooms in Darby Street in Harwich, I believe it's number thirteen. Could your Dr. Devereaux go there?"

"Never fear, he'll find him and tell him what's happened."

"Perhaps Charles can come back here."

"If you like, although I don't think you should be moved, at least not for a day or two. I have no doubt Dr. Collier would agree on that."

"Nevertheless, I would like to see him."

"And you shall, but at the moment I think we'd best have no more questions. What you need more than conversation or visitors is a good night's sleep."

Reaching into his vest pocket, he took out a small vial. Holding it in his left hand, he removed the stopper from the carafe of water standing on the night table, poured a quantity into a glass and, uncorking the vial, carefully added a few drops of the contents.

"What is that?"

"A sleeping draught. Perfectly harmless. I merely want to make certain that you sleep through the rest of the night without discomfort."

"I'm exhausted. I'll sleep."

"Take it, please." He held the glass before her lips. "Drink it all."

She hesitated, he smiled encouragement and she took the glass and drank. Within seconds a drowsy feeling took possession of her, her eyelids becoming heavy, the doctor's face looming above her beginning to waver as if turning to liquid.

And she slept. She passed the night without nightmares and awoke to the sun streaming in through the window drenching the counterpane with its golden warmth. Gingerly, she tried to raise upward to test her injured shoulder but found to her disappointment that it was little improved, although the throbbing pain in both her shoulder and her head had dulled somewhat. Her body ached all over and her mouth was as dry as dust. Lying back on the pillow, she cleared her throat and called aloud for Alma, but it wasn't until nearly ten minutes had gone by that the woman appeared, leading Alison to surmise that she had not heard her and had only looked into the room because she happened to be passing the door.

She went away and returned bringing a soft-boiled egg in a delicate bone china cup girdled with gold filigree, warm toast and jam, and a cup of exceptionally strong tea. After Alison had eaten, she felt stronger and began assailing Alma with all sorts of questions. Had Cousin Charles been told of the accident? Was he coming to the house? Where was Dr. Maartens now? Was he coming to see her?

To all of which Alma only shook her head and shrugged. Evidently the woman knew nothing about Dr. Devereaux's late night quest for Charles nor anything else of what had transpired while she, Alison, had slept, if indeed anything at all had transpired. Alison turned the conversation to Barringer House and Dr. Maartens.

"We came here a year ago," explained Alma.

"From where?"

"Albany, in New York. This is a strange house. It was owned by the master of a sailing ship and was used for smuggling, so they say." Her eyes widened and she leaned over the bed and pointed downward. "Below in the rock is a cave. There's a secret stairway that goes down from the cellar to a landing. Small boats were able to go into the cave and tie up underneath. Smugglers and pirates yes, and a bloody history, murder and worse. He was hanged, you know."

"Mr. Barringer?"

"Captain Barringer. It's said he murdered his mistress in cold blood, cut her to pieces and flung them to the sharks. She was unfaithful to him. Portuguese she was, and beautiful."

"You heard . . ."

"I saw. To this day her picture hangs above the fireplace downstairs."

Alma rambled on, warming to her subject, and her listener could hardly tell where fact ended and fantasy began. If there were a grain of truth in what the woman said, however, Barringer House certainly boasted an unusual history. And yet neither the house nor its past interested Alison, but rather Maartens and his group — Devereaux, Otto, Nurse Raphael and any others who lived there. The scene in the cemetery kept coming back to her, and if she were subtle and clever perhaps she might elicit an explanation from Alma.

The woman was as willing to talk about her employer as she had been to talk about the house, although Alison noted that she took the trouble to close the door before beginning.

"Possessed he is."

"Of what?"

"He has the power. Of life and death."

"You don't say."

"It's true, true as God made me." She made the sign of

the cross and nodded vigorously. "You wouldn't smirk like that if you knew what I know about Hendrik Maartens."

"The power of life and death."

Alma's eyes reflected alarm. Suddenly she seemed afraid to continue, reluctant to probe into subjects forbidden discussion. And yet the temptation proved too strong to resist. She bit the back of her index finger to steel herself and resumed: "I've seen him bring a body back to life!"

Alison laughed. "Forgive me, Alma, I'm not laughing at you, really I'm not. It's just that the idea is so . . . so fantastic."

"Fantastic, is it? I've seen it, I tell you, with these two eyes! A body dead and buried in its grave, dug up, brought to this very house, laid out as if at the wake and words spoken."

"What words?"

"Not by him."

"By who then?"

"The old one, his mother. Do you know how old she is?"

"How could I possibly know how old she is? I've never even laid eyes on her."

"A hundred and nineteen. God strike me dead if I lie one year!"

"You mean she says she's a hundred and nineteen."

"She is. You doubting Thomas, how old do you think he is?"

"Dr. Maartens? Fifty-eight, sixty, no more than that."

"He's eighty-nine years old."

"That's ridiculous. I've seen the man, his hair, his complexion . . ."

"Eighty-nine. I told you, he has the power . . ."

"Of life and death, I know. Does he also have the power of slowing down the aging process, stopping it? If he does, he's surely missing his calling. He should be traveling about plying his trade, keeping the great old men and women of the world from getting any older."

Alma shot to her feet. The fear had fled her eyes, replaced by indignation. "You mock me."

"I'm not mocking you. It's just that . . ."

"It's just the truth. Say what you like, you'll see! Before you leave this house you'll find out! A dog, its head cut clean off and placed on a piece of glass. Snarling and barking as if it never felt the knife. And no blood, not a drop. And what would you say to a white candle burning and dripping not wax, but blood as red as yours and mine! I've seen them, I tell you. And Nurse Raphael, wait till you see her and what Dr. Maartens did to her in that infernal room below! The dead come to life, he can make it happen. He's done it! Bodies cold as ice breathing, speaking . . . You'll see! You'll wish you hadn't!"

Seizing the breakfast tray, she swept to the door, wrenched it open and leaving it wide in her wake, disappeared down the corridor.

Alison lay staring at the ceiling, Alma's words ringing in her ears. This house, this room, these people, she wanted no more of them. The old woman's ramblings had not really upset her, taking them as she did with a grain of salt, except the business of the dead coming to life. That had to be tied in with what she had seen in the cemetery the night before. And yet whether it was or not it was not nearly as important as her own welfare and what the next few hours held for her. Let Maartens and Otto and all of them steal all the corpses they pleased, she could care less at this point.

She must leave Barringer House, that very day, that very hour if she was able to. She tested her shoulder, flinching with the pain, and throwing back the bedclothes swung both legs over the side. The floor was like ice against her bare feet, but steadying herself with both fists she tried to rise. No sooner had she straightened than dizziness seized her and she gulped for air as the room began to swim.

Getting back into the bed, she drew the covers into place and putting Alma and her grisly narrative out of her mind, turned her thoughts to her situation. If only the doctor would come and talk with her, assure her that Devereaux had contacted Charles. But then, if he had, where was Charles, why hadn't he come to her? It was her mother who really worried her. Lying there practically as helpless as she, she yearned to speak with her, calm her fears and persuade her that everything would be all right, that the shock of daddy's death would pass in time, that the days filled with sorrow and emptiness would not go on forever.

As she studied the ceiling and the windows looking out on the bright, clear blue sky, time passed like a snail tracing its way across a garden floor. Each time she looked at her watch the minute hand seemed hardly to have moved.

At noon, Dr. Maartens appeared in the doorway. She didn't hear his footsteps and the sudden sight of him startled her. He looked exhausted, as if he had been up all night. His hair was mussed, his sleeves carelessly rolled up and his eyes, naturally red-rimmed, looked like two open wounds. When he spoke, his voice betrayed his fatigue, but the same friendly tone was there, the warmth and cordiality.

"And how are we feeling this morning?"

"Much better. I think I'm well enough to leave."

"That's good news."

"Doctor, was Dr. Devereaux able to contact my cousin in Harwich?"

"Oh yes, he told him everything and your cousin promised to get in touch with your mother in Pittsburgh right away."

"Philadelphia."

"Of course."

He was lying. Lie was written all over his face. But why, to what purpose? At that, what difference did it make? Her mind was made up. She would leave this place if she had to drag herself to the door and into the carriage!

"I appreciate it," she said, "more than I can say. And I am sorry for all the inconvenience I've caused you."

"No inconvenience whatsoever. Accidents will happen. Practically in front of our gate this time. It's good to know you're mending, though."

"I really am."

"Alma brought you breakfast."

"I ate every bite."

"A good sign. You look better. How's the shoulder?"

"Much better."

"And your head?"

"Good as new."

"No pain?" The red eyes searched her face, reading beyond her responses to his questions.

"Just a little. If Alma will bring me my clothes and someone will call a carriage . . ."

"My, my, we are in a rush, aren't we?"

"My mother . . ."

"Yes, of course. But let's both be sure you're fit before we send you on your way. You've a long journey ahead of you. And what sort of doctor would I be if I took my patients' words for their condition? You, young lady, are more restless than you are recovered."

"No, really, I'm just fine."

"We shall see." He took her face between both hands and

stared into her eyes. "Eyes clear, good sign that." Letting both hands drop, he took hold of hers. The coldness of his touch on her face and her hands sent a chill up her spine, but she did not free her hands. "Suppose you get out of bed and walk to the door. Do you think you can?"

"Of course."

She would do it, without betraying dizziness, or going pale. Taking a deep breath, she threw off the covers and placed both feet on the floor. Pushing upward, the same dizziness took hold of her and she teetered slightly, her hand going back down to the mattress for support. Straightening, she began to walk toward the door. Only six steps, less . . . but even before she had calculated the distance, the room began to whirl, her eyes swinging up to the ceiling, and she dissolved in his arms.

He helped her back into bed, tucking her in and waggling a disapproving finger.

"We're not as well as we think we are. Let's give it one more day."

"But . . ."

"Just one."

He smiled, turned and left the room.

Alma brought her lunch, cold meatloaf, brown bread and butter and more tea, so strong that it set her teeth on edge. But she drank every drop, knowing that she would need all the nourishment she could get to speed her recovery, to get out of the house, into a carriage and onto the train that would take her hundreds of miles from there. Alma spoke hardly a word, her thin lips clamped tightly together as if she did not trust herself to open them. Her feelings were obviously hurt and she wore a look that said very plainly, Miss Doubter, you're in for a few surprises.

She neither wanted nor needed surprises. Enough had

happened to her in the past few hours to last her half a lifetime. She thanked Alma for the meal and the woman took the tray and went away.

Throughout the afternoon, she tried to sleep but the nervous strain that had taken over her body would not permit her to do so. Gulls wheeled back and forth outside the window shrieking noisily, the wind came up and chased itself around the house, slipping through the eaves and now and then rattling the windows; and the snail of time moved more and more slowly.

Just before her tenth birthday she had contracted measles—from Grace Swan, her very best friend. The three weeks she had spent in bed had been like three months and looking back on it now she could remember times when it was all she could do to keep from screaming out loud, so bored was she.

But that all-too-memorable imprisonment between sheets had been spent in the comfort of the knowledge that she was among loved ones, that all her needs were being taken care of, and that she had nothing to fear from anyone or anything.

How discouragingly different this was. Examining her situation, she almost believed she might never again see the outside world. But that was patently absurd. Surely her imagination was going too far, and Alma's wild assertions were obscuring her reason and common sense. Then, too, perhaps she was being overly concerned about her mother. After all, wasn't Lydia, the maid, there to take care of her? Wasn't Lydia capable and responsible? And didn't Dr. Monroe look in every day?

Actually, her own Dr. Maartens was taking excellent care of her. Were she less suspicious and more objective about her situation she would have to concede that his attention to her recovery, his insistence that she be well enough to travel before she be allowed to leave was certainly all in her own best interests. Indeed, what else could he do in such a circumstance?

All of which would have gone down easily, but for his lies about Charles.

It was either her raw determination to recover as quickly as possible or her increasing distaste for her surroundings that prompted the change, but by late afternoon she actually began feeling stronger. Then, just after five o'clock something happened which practically pulled her out of her bed.

Lying dozing, she was suddenly aware of voices, a man and a woman arguing close by. Pushing herself up on both elbows, she decided that the sounds were coming from near the cabriole-table. She made it to the table without too much trouble and steadying herself against it, looked down at the floor. A few inches to the left of the rear leg, she spied a hole through which the two voices were coming. Immediately, she recognized Alma and the doctor.

"What did you tell her?"

"Nothing, doctor, not a word."

"Come now, Alma, I know you. Your tongue never stops waggling. I suppose you filled her head full of your fantasies, all the nonsense you steal from your nightmares . . ."

"I told her nothing, only about the house and the legends."

"Nothing about me, of course."

"Oh no, I swear on my mother's grave."

"You usually do, when you're lying. You lie so obviously, Alma, the words come out of you and your eyes roll up in your head announcing your untruthfulness. But you know that, don't you, I've told you that time and again."

"I told her nothing about you, about any of us."

"See that you don't!" His tone was cold, the threat implicit. "She's here purely by accident. I don't want her here, I want her packed up and gone as soon as she's able to travel. Hopefully tomorrow. But while she's with us, what goes on in this house is none of her affair, do you understand me?"

"Yes, sir."

"You'll hold your tongue if you know what's good for you. Now, get back to your kitchen and stay there!"

"Yes, yes . . ."

Alison returned to her bed with mixed feelings, her anxiety somewhat relieved by Maartens' announcement that he wanted her out of the house as soon as possible, but her curiosity was measurably increased.

After she had finished her evening meal and Alma had taken away the things, Maartens appeared with his sleeping draught.

"Do you think I need it tonight, doctor?"

"I would prefer that you take it."

"Whatever you say." She accepted the vial and looked on as he poured her a glass of water. Then she herself poured three drops, as he had done the previous night, into the glass, corking the vial and handing it back to him. She would show him that she was much improved, and that she was not at all reluctant to down the laudanum or whatever it was he was giving her. It was imperative that he believe she had every confidence in him. "It's only seven," she said, "may I take it at eight o'clock?"

"Of course. Pleasant dreams."

He went away, closing the door behind him. At once she got out of bed and, crossing to the window, tossed the contents of the glass into the sea below. Then she refilled the glass to the identical level from the carafe beside the candle on the nightstand.

She needed none of his medicine. She fell asleep within the hour and was deep in a pleasant dream when she suddenly awoke. The sound of voices was coming up through the hole in the floor. They were low, and even when she got down on hands and knees beside the hole and listened, it was difficult to make out what was being said. Once again, however, Dr. Maartens was one of them.

Presently they left the room, their voices fading. Who the two strangers there, what they were doing at the house at that time of night she couldn't imagine. But the more she dwelled on it, the more curious she became.

Moving to her door, she eased it open and ventured out into the corridor. There was no sound of any sort from downstairs. The corridor stretched left and right, illuminated by sconces on either side. She started to the left toward a forbidding-looking door at the far end. Walking easily and without dizziness, she came within a few feet of the door when suddenly she stopped short and stared at it. Its solid presence frightened her, as if some indescribable horror lay beyond it, like a cat crouching to spring at her. This house, this bleak and gloomy monument to a sailing master's lifelong struggle with the masterless sea, this timeworn catch-all of legends and mysteries perched on its rock overlooking the restless deep . . . shunned by the world, left to its own devices . . . was suddenly as loathsome to her as some nameless crawling thing.

The door was before her. Urged on by some strange force, she lifted her hand, reaching for the knob to turn it. The iron touching her fingertips brought a cold and invisible hand to the nape of her neck. Steeling herself, she turned it, opening the door.

To her relief, the way beyond was empty and lit by a single sconce only. Four doors lined the wall to the left, but to the right was a heavy railing. Pausing beside it, she looked down.

The scene that greeted her eyes surprised her. It appeared as if some pagan ritual was about to take place. Against a large, dark blue velvet drape covering the far wall entirely stood two large wrought-iron candleholders, at least eight feet tall. Between them, her hands folded in her lap, sat the oldest woman Alison had ever seen, her bones bunched together in her skin, her flesh drained of the juices of life, her face a mass of wrinkles so deeply gouged by the years that her features were all but obscured in their folds. Her lips moved, but no sound escaped them. She was sitting in a low chair, straight-backed with wide armrests, the sort found in a child's bedroom, and her birdlike body was wrapped in the folds of her black robes covered from shoulder to hem with silver designs.

Directly before her stood a long empty table. A middle-aged man, broad-shouldered and vigorous looking, and a woman whose head barely came to his shoulder were seated at the opposite end of the table facing the old woman down its length. The two were well-dressed, the woman in an expensive brocade dress with a string of pearls about her throat. Her back was to Alison, but even without seeing her face, it was obvious that she was upset. Her narrow shoulders jerked and she repeatedly went to her eyes with a handkerchief balled in her hand. As Alison watched, the man sitting at her left reached across and took the woman's left hand comfortingly, whispering to her. Incense burned in brass bowls on stands at the four corners of the scene and a line of candles, not nearly as tall as those on either side of the old woman in the chair, burned brightly behind the couple seated almost directly under Alison. There was an unearthly quality about the scene that repelled her as she gazed down upon it, as if some strange forbidden game was about to begin. The old woman looked to be more dead than alive and it was almost as if she had come back from the grave bringing word from beyond it, to reveal it and return.

Even as Alison stood staring down, the door at the left opened and a man and a woman in the uniform of a nurse, whom she assumed to be Nurse Raphael, entered wheeling a cart carrying a closed casket. The wheels squeaked absurdly as it was rolled across the dark maroon carpet toward the table. At sight of the casket, the woman in the brocade dress cried out and the man quickly grabbed her by the arm to keep her from rising from her chair. She looked at him pleadingly and he said something quietly to her, and as he turned his face to speak, Alison could clearly see the tension and suffering in the tautness of his cheek muscles and the set of his jaw.

Dr. Maartens appeared behind the nurse and the man. He gestured to the man and moving swiftly to either end of the wheeled conveyance, they shifted the casket onto the table. Maartens opened it, revealing the corpse of a young woman. At sight of her, the woman looking on cried out again. Alison stifled a gasp, grasping the railing for support as she did so. At that moment, the scene was blotted out as a hand closed over her face, covering her eyes and mouth.

Her heart pounded, she screamed silently and fainted.

3

The coach plunged headlong down the hill, gathering speed as it went, careening from side to side, threatening to overturn at any moment. Suddenly it stopped dead, the rear wheels lifting high, the cumbersome vehicle crashing down on its right side, toppling over upside down. Her head struck the doorpost and instantly she lost consciousness.

She awoke to discover a man, a grotesque creature lifting her bodily out of the shattered wreckage of the coach. Powerful arms carried her across the sodden ground, the rain pelting her in the face as she stared at the starless heavens, her head bobbing like a rag doll's. She raised it with effort, and her eyes wandered to the face of the man carrying her. It was ugly beyond description, the corners of the heavy-lipped mouth upturned in a leer. She cried out and the wind rose in response, roaring defiance even as the rain increased in intensity. Within seconds, the man's long strides had brought them to a graveside where a second man, a saturnine-looking fellow, stood leaning on his shovel and holding a lamp aloft. The rain ran down his face, collecting at the point of his narrow chin and dropping off into the open casket in the grave at his feet.

The man carrying her bent over to place her in the casket. She kicked and screamed and the second man began laughing wildly. She clawed at the bigger man's face, but despite her resistance down she went into the casket and the lid, its hinges grinding, was slowly lowered, cutting off the rain, blocking out sight of the black sky overhead and the two grinning faces, closing with a dull thud.

She screamed, the sound striking the lid inches from her face and rebounding hollowly. And she began gasping for air as the muffled sound of shovels digging became audible and the dirt, lumped by the rain, pounded down upon her.

She woke up gasping for breath, her body covered with perspiration, droplets of it stinging her eyes. Getting up, she reeled to the window and by the light of the moon looked at her watch. It was after four o'clock. No sound came from below through the hole in the floor. Curious, she crossed to the door and tried it. But as she suspected, it was locked.

Getting back into bed, she turned over the earlier events in her mind. What was it all about? The two strangers and the dead girl, lovely blond hair surrounding her waxen features, eyes and lips sealed, the air of death hanging about her like mist over a meadow . . . Reflecting on the episode, asking herself questions she could not answer, she soon fell back asleep, lulled by the sea wind moaning outside the window, and hanging by a slender thread to one consolation; physically she was much improved, although the same could not be said for the state of her nerves.

She awoke shortly after eight, feeling tired, but relieved to see the light of day. She had not been awake more than a few minutes when a key sounded in the door and it opened, revealing Dr. Maartens carrying her breakfast tray. Quelling the urge to question him about the previous night, she returned his greeting cordially and let him assume the burden of initiating conversation.

"You look much better, my dear. Please, don't stand on ceremony. Eat your breakfast before it gets cold."

He talked about the weather and the speed with which

the roads were drying up in the wake of the storm. He talked of his boyhood love of the sea and the need to ready the house for winter, but to all of this she only half listened, until he got around to asking how she felt.

"I'm leaving today, doctor."

His eyes narrowed and he turned his head toward the window, his thick muscular neck reddening slightly. He pretended to be preoccupied by two beady-eyed terns wheeling about outside carving circles in the cloudless blue sky.

"I do appreciate your hospitality. You and Alma have been very kind to me. If I can leave here by noon I'm sure there's a train . . ."

"I would rather you stay on."

"But I'm perfectly . . ."

"What you stumbled upon last night was none of your affair, we both know that. Unfortunately, your curiosity has created a problem and until we can resolve that problem one way or another, I'll have to ask you to continue on as our guest."

"Guest or prisoner?"

"Prisoner?"

She studied him archly. He has missed his calling. He should have been an actor; the raised eyebrow, the feigned surprise, the sudden alteration of tone to suit the new mood were all there. But she was too annoyed to be entertained by his performance.

"Dr. Maartens, I apologize for eavesdropping. I had no right to, curiosity is no excuse. But I saw nothing of consequence, certainly nothing to tell me what was going on."

"Come now, Miss Collier, you're not stupid. You saw a young girl in a casket surrounded by a group of people and you have no idea what we were doing? Let's be honest. You have a very good idea what we were doing. And the moment you're outside this house you'll go running to your cousin or to the police and tell them."

"You can't hold me, I'm leaving . . ."

"No!" The single word was a heavy door closing, bolting. He shook his head and smiled at her, an unpleasant smirk that said all too plainly that whatever guarantee of silence she offered, it would be unacceptable. "Why don't we discuss it later? Your eggs are getting cold."

"I'm not hungry, thank you, and I prefer to talk about it now. If you force me to stay here against my will you'll regret it. Kidnapping is a serious crime."

"Indeed it is, but this is hardly kidnapping."

"I'm leaving here, if I have to walk to the station!"

Sighing, he got up from the side of the bed and without speaking walked out of the room, relocking the door, her protests, loud and empty, following him out.

That settled it! She would bide her time, wait until darkness, until they were all asleep, sneak out and walk to Brunswick, even if it meant sleeping in that smelly waiting room in the station until morning! Better yet, she'd go to Harwich and the hospital, find cousin Charles, tell all, and let him put the police onto the mad doctor and his tribe. She would board her train and go home.

Maartens wouldn't touch a hair of her head, that was certain. He'd told her nothing regarding the ceremony, and yet in a sense he'd told all. His first thought had been the police, which had to mean that whatever it was they were up to was illegal. Certainly if the little she had witnessed was within the law he would hardly be concerned about her telling anyone. Or would he? It was all so confusing . . .

Alma. The power of life and death. She had said it straightfaced, with a gravity that verged on the ridiculous. Was there a grain of truth in it? The corpse of the young girl, the two strangers, probably her father and mother . . .

And Maartens was actually going to attempt to bring her back to life? Incredible! Absolute nonsense. Anyone with half an eye could see she was dead. As if the old woman's muttering, the doctor's bag of tricks, or the incense burning could breathe life into the poor thing!

Obviously Maartens had brought her her breakfast tray to tell her the bad news in person. Likely she'd seen the last of Alma; the woman talked too much and Maartens had no doubt decided to keep the two of them rooms apart. And it was surely Otto who had grabbed her from behind, he was the only one of the occupants of the house not taking part in the grisly drama below the railing.

Very well, if this was the way Maartens wanted it, so be it. But, he was right, once she was out she would tell the world what she'd seen, shout it from the housetops! Everyone with hearing would know of Dr. Hendrik Maartens and his games played with corpses.

But reflecting on the situation, she was forced to admit that she really hadn't seen very much. Otto had taken care of that. Then, too, why pry further into the ghastly business? Perhaps it would be wiser to get out and forget it. Put it behind her forever, with Maine, and Barringer House and the lot of them.

Finishing breakfast, she set the tray on the edge of the nightstand and got out of bed. Her shoulder was sore, but the nagging pain which had afflicted it earlier had gone away and her head no longer ached. She went to the armoire standing at the wall opposite the window and opened it. Hanging neatly from a cloth-covered hanger was her dress, her shoes side by side under it. Her coat and bags were there, too. At least when she left she wouldn't freeze to death in the chill October air. She was tempted to get dressed, but Maartens might come back anytime and if he were to see her dressed, he'd know what she was up to, as if he didn't already suspect. She had no way of gauging her chances of escape, but attempting to do so in the dead of night promised to minimize the risk. If she could make it to the front door without raising anyone, she'd get to the main road and head either way until she came to a sign indicating Harwich or Brunswick, anywhere!

Night was interminably long in coming, the garden snail plodding along. Unable to nap, she sat by the window all afternoon looking down and watching lobster boats wallow about the sea, with now and then a clipper ship appearing, heading out for deep water. At long last the sun went down, the welcome mantle of night replacing its glow. It would be a hunter's night, the sky blackening and filling with stars and the full moon strewing silver over the restless water below. Dr. Maartens came by at seven-thirty to take away her dinner tray brought earlier by Otto, sight of whom sent a chill up her spine. The doctor was as friendly and as charming as usual, but there was an icy edge to his tone, part threat and part concern, as he lectured her briefly on the evils of eavesdropping. Then he went off on a different tack, in a too-obvious attempt to unburden his conscience. To Alison, the impression was that he was basically a good man caught in a circumstance, a situation of questionable morality, prompting him to rationalization and apology.

"I am neither a blacksmith nor a scholar. I am a doctor of medicine and a surgeon of no mean skill, if I do say so myself. And knowing whereof I speak, I must tell you this. There are many practices engaged in by medical men like myself and Dr. Devereaux which are beyond the understanding of the layman. Call them investigations, experiments, anything you please, they go on. And because they do and always will, doctors have no easy time of it. We labor in our vineyard of life and death under the eyes of public and private critics who have neither the training nor the intellect to understand what we're doing. And because they don't understand or they're unwilling to give us the benefit of their doubt, they raise a hue and cry, point the finger and scream stop. Those who condemn do so innocently—with all the good intentions in the world—or jealously, out of pure malice, stirring up their mischief simply to satisfy themselves. Either way, they lose sight of one salient fact. The healer builds, he does not destroy. With his oath, he takes on a lifelong dedication to his art, and he'll allow nothing to stand in the way of his efforts to improve that art. No physician worth the name would hesitate to do what he can to better the art, to make his contribution, however small, to help eliminate sickness and disease, to prolong life, to delay death . . ."

"Forgive me, doctor, but is all this really necessary? Or is it simply that you feel a need to justify whatever it is you're up to? If you do, I must ask you not to trouble yourself. What you do is your own business and I've already apologized for my curiosity, understandable though it may have been. I heard voices, I investigated. Time passes very slowly in this room, the hours are long and boring."

"I can understand that."

"Sending Otto up to frighten me out of my wits really wasn't called for. He might have tapped me on the shoulder and asked me to leave instead of dragging me off like . . . like . . ."

"I'm sorry."

"I'm a good deal sorrier about being kept here against my will!"

"It's either that or I let you leave, which as your doctor . . ."

"I can't believe you're that concerned about my health anymore."

"I most certainly am."

"Then when I arrive home I shall write you a letter telling you exactly how I feel."

"You're not leaving, not today."

"Then when, next week, next month? This is becoming more serious by the hour, you're getting in deeper and you know it. There's a very simple solution. Fetch me a carriage and allow me to leave now, right now, and we can both forget this entire matter."

Maartens hesitated, his brow furrowing, his lower lip pushing up against the upper one, as if weighing her words. But instead of responding, he tried to turn the conversation to other matters, the reason for her trip to Maine, her father's illness. She ignored him, avoiding his eyes and staring at the armoire. At length he turned to preparing her sleeping draught, handing it to her. Reaching across the nightstand, she poured it into the water carafe.

"Thank you all the same, I don't need it tonight."

"As you please."

He shrugged and left. But no sooner was he out the door than she began to regret her show of spirit. If there had been any hope in his mind that she wouldn't tell what she had seen, that hope was now dispelled. So be it. She'd started out trying to play the innocent and he'd seen through it immediately, why shouldn't she speak her mind? He had no right holding her, people were put behind bars every day for lesser offenses. Damn the man! Damn his red eyes and sticky manner, his stubbornness and calculated deceit! She would show him!

She stayed awake until after eleven, then getting out her reticule, took out the small carved Chinese box containing her hairpins and needle and thread. Using a large hairpin like a pair of tongs, she went to work on the lock. Again and again she caught it and tried to turn it over and release the bolt, but it slipped off, unable to carry the weight of it.

Adding two more pins to the one she was using, she inserted them in the keyhole and managed to release the bolt first try. The sound of it throwing back was lilting music. Relocking it at once, she got back into bed. There was no sense leaving the door open for her later departure. If Maartens or Otto or anyone else prowling the outside corridor were to try it and find it unlocked, they'd probably put a chair up against it and that would be that.

At midnight the sound of voices came floating up through the opening in the floor. She could not be altogether certain, but it sounded like the man and the woman she had heard the previous night, along with Maartens and one other man. Another "ceremony" was scheduled. Of all the luck! So let them go at it, she wanted no part of their preposterous games, not at the risk of Otto again sneaking up and manhandling her. If it took an hour or even two, she would wait patiently and when they were done and the house quieted down for the night she would make her move.

The voices went away after a few minutes, which meant that the group was on its way to the large room below the railing. The old woman would begin her mumbling and the corpse would be wheeled out. There was something so wretched and so immoral about it. The dead were so helpless in the hands of the living, wheeled about like tea things on a wagon, mumbo jumboed over, fiddled and fussed with, it was disgusting! Ghouls they were, all of them, no better than Otto and his friend robbing the grave!

But for all her intentions, for all her determination, she

could not control her curiosity. Getting dressed, she unlocked the door without any difficulty and closing it behind her, made her way down the corridor. Reaching the railing, she was surprised to see that although all the props had been assembled and the candles lit, none of the players had come onto the scene. Taking advantage of the delay, she cast about for a place to hide from where she might see Otto coming before he saw her. She tried one of the doors across from the railing and finding it locked, took out her improvised pick and opened it with little difficulty. Inside the room, moonlight flooded in through both windows facing the sea, revealing half-filled bookcases and crates containing books still unpacked. Other than the bookcases standing against all four walls, the room was sparsely furnished, a bare table, one chair, and under the window to the left, a reading stand, a large volume lying open upon it. She crossed to the window to look out upon the sea. Under the sill, the cliff dropped sheer to the water below as it did under the window of her own room. One after another, the waves raced up to the wall of stone, exploding against it. As she stood by the window, her eyes fell to the book on the stand. Slips of paper marked four or five pages. She lifted the cover to see the title: *Exploring the Arctic* by Dr. Costigan. Aimlessly, she began leafing through it, reaching the first paper mark and reading the underlined words:

> "Nearly all our party, as well the rescuers as the rescued, were tossing in their sick-bunks, some frozen, others undergoing amputations, several with dreadful premonitions of tetanus. I was myself among the first to be about; the necessities of the others claimed it of me.
>
> "Early in the morning of the 7th I was awakened by a sound from Goddard's throat, one of those the most

frightful and ominous that ever startle a physician's ear. The lock-jaw had seized him, that dark visitant whose foreshadowing were on so many of us. His symptoms marched rapidly to their result: he died on the 8th of April. We placed him the next day in his coffin, and forming a rude but heartfull procession, bore him over the broken ice and up the steep side of the ice-foot to Malverne Island. We read the service for the burial of the dead, sprinkling over him snow for dust, and repeated the Lord's Prayer; and then, icing up again the opening in the walls we had made to admit the coffin, left him in his narrow house."

Turning to the next slip she read:

"*Deo volente,* I will be luckier tomorrow. I am going to take my long Kentucky rifle, the kayack, and Esquimaux harpoon with its attached line and bladder, *naligeit* and *awahtok,* and a pair of large snow-shoes to boot. My plan this time is to kneel where the ice is unsafe, resting my weight on the broad surface of the snow-shoes, Hans following astride of his kayack, as a sort of life-preserver in case of breaking in. If I am fortunate enough to stalk within gun-range, Hans will take to the water and secure the game before it sinks. We will be gone for some days probably, tenting it in the open air; but our sick men—that is to say, all of us—are languishing for fresh meat. And if we do not obtain it we are surely doomed."

A third of the way through the book as she turned the pages rapidly, a loose paper suddenly flew out, sailing to the floor. It had been folded once. She picked it up to slip it back between the pages, pausing to examine it. It was cheap writing paper, with an item clipped from a newspaper neatly pasted to it:

> Albany, December 4th. Police of this city are searching for Dr. Louis Hoorn wanted for questioning in the death under mysterious circumstances of Eleanor Lyons of 118 Berwick Street. It has been reported that the deceased was a patient of Dr. Hoorn's until the night of her disappearance.
>
> The missing physician is described as being of medium height with dark hair, and an unusually pale complexion. He is approximately 60 years old. Anyone with information regarding this man is asked to contact Sgt. Thomas Burkett at the Lower Broadway Station House.

Refolding the paper and placing it back in the book, she riffled the pages back to the front cover and closed it. Dr. Louis Hoorn, Albany. Alma had mentioned Albany as their previous residence. "Death under mysterious circumstances," what better reason for leaving town? So she had underestimated Dr. Hendrik Maartens, Dr. Louis Hoorn, whatever his real name . . .

Had he murdered that girl? Or had he subjected her to some experiment in the interests of "improving the healing arts"? But why would he save the newspaper clipping? Once more she opened the book. In green ink in the upper left hand corner of the inside cover was a name: John B. Devereaux, M.D.

Dr. Costigan's *Exploring the Arctic* was Dr. Devereaux's, his book, his clipping, report of an incident well worth preserving. To hold over Maartens' head? A weapon of defense to be cached away until needed?

The door at her back was ajar and through it came the sound of people entering the room below. Going to the door, standing beside it, she could see the scene below except for the audience at the near end of the table and the candles behind them, the angle of view being cut off by the corridor floor. Bringing the chair up to the door, she positioned it and sat down holding the door open barely three inches with her left foot. Her better judgment reproached her for delaying her flight simply to satisfy her curiosity, but she rationalized her decision, persuading herself that she couldn't leave anything as long as the others were up and about.

The performance began in the same manner as the night before, Nurse Raphael and Devereaux wheeling out the corpse and Maartens and Devereaux placing the casket on the table where it was opened. Maartens stood with his hand on the lid and addressed his audience.

"Again I apologize for what happened last night. My mother is very old and very weak. The effort she makes is extremely exhausting for one of her advanced years, added to which she has been suffering from a disorder of the throat recently and is still not fully recovered from the effects of it. I can only ask you to share our patience. There is, unfortunately, no guarantee of success in what we are about to undertake. We must all of us accept that. We shall try everything within our limited powers, and hope and pray that we can bring it about, but if we fail to do so . . ."

He made a theatrical gesture of helplessness and looked to Nurse Raphael who moved to a tall metal cabinet at the right of the door and took out a small glass bottle half-filled with white powder and three stethoscopes hanging beside the bottle. Keeping one of the instruments for herself, she handed the other two to Maartens and Devereaux in turn, then moving to the nearest tall wrought-iron candlestand, took a handful of powder from the bottle and tossed it up onto the flame. A puff of purple smoke rose, immediately changing the orange flame to purple and casting a weird glow over the room. She repeated the gesture with the candle on the other side, then returned the bottle to the cabinet.

Maartens' mother lifted her head slowly and, raising both hands, began speaking aloud in a language Alison did not understand. Her voice came reedily from deep in her throat, each succeeding sentence requiring increased effort of will for her to summon the power to go on:

"Eerish myoco lassa. Ninthinta . . ."

On and on she babbled, her frail diminutive body weaving from side to side, her face twisted with strain, the silver designs on her robes catching the purple light of the candles and giving off light of their own. No move was made toward the dead girl until the purple glow vanished and the natural candlelight returned. As if one cue, Maartens and Devereaux approached the casket and, freeing the lower half of the cover, set it on the floor at the foot of the table. Now the shrouded corpse was fully revealed, only the head exposed, the sealed eyes stone-like, the golden hair neatly arranged around the sweet, unblemished and colorless face. Nurse Raphael left the room, returning at once wheeling a small table on which bottles and flasks and surgical instruments were laid out, all but obscuring the white cloth covering the table. It was positioned beside the casket, Maartens moving to it. Opening a tall bottle of red liquid, he dipped a cotton swab into it and, rubbing it across the lips of the dead girl, stood watching as it dried in place. Other actions followed, turning back the folds of the shroud to expose her throat, Devereaux examining the jugular vein with his stethoscope, straightening and shaking his head at Maartens, and Maartens himself bending over the girl to examine her face and the flesh of her right hand with a small glass held close to his right eye.

For more than an hour by her watch, Alison looked on as the two men and the woman went through all sorts of procedures, using the ingredients and the instruments on the small table. And while they worked, the old woman continued her chanting, lowering her clawlike hands with increasing frequency only to raise them again as if appealing to some unseen power to assist her efforts.

"Missaga norra des. Lakano creese . . ."

Her brow glistened with beads of perspiration as she went on, then abruptly she stopped, her hands dropping to her lap, her chin falling to her narrow chest. Maartens and Devereaux hastened to her and while Devereaux ministered to her, giving her a breath of ammonium carbonate and opening the clasp of her robes at the throat to give her needed air, Maartens turned to the casket and closed it.

"No!" The woman watching, unseen by Alison up to now, started out of her chair, coming forward into view. Wringing her hands, she cried out. "Please . . . don't please! Keep trying . . ."

Dr. Maartens looked at her sympathetically, then glanced back at Dr. Devereaux and his mother.

"She's all right, Dr. Maartens, she wants to go on."

"I don't think it wise . . ."

"I am all right, Louis," said the old woman with surprising firmness.

Maartens hesitated, shrugged and reopened the casket, the woman returning to her chair and the ceremony resuming. To Alison looking on from her place of concealment, the entire performance had long since passed the point of mere fascination. It had become at once the most gruesome and the most heartless sham ever conceived, a raree macabre straight out of a penny dreadful. What amazed her more than anything was that the man and woman should deliberately subject themselves to such obvious fakery. To think that they sat there actually believing that Maartens and Devereaux and the old woman could possibly succeed in bringing the girl back from the other side! How long she had been dead there was no way of knowing, but dead she was and dead she would be forever, as lifeless and immobile as stone. How could Maartens prey on these people's superstitions, their false and baseless hopes for a miracle? How could he take their hearts in his hands like cups and fill them with disappointment, with deliberate and certain reaffirmation of their tragic loss? What manner of monster was he? What quirk of mind, what prod in his ego impelled him to such conscienceless behavior? She wanted to scream at him, at all of them. But instead she held her anger in check and continued to watch.

She began to wish that the whole business would be done with, that the couple suffering their inevitable disappointment and with Maartens' apologies in their ears would be on their way, and their host and his accomplices gone to bed and asleep for what remained of the night.

By a quarter to three she began to have difficulty keeping her eyes open. She longed for a drink of water and the chance to splash a few drops on her face, but she could not tear herself away from the spectacle continuing to unfold below the railing. Nurse Raphael came around the casket and filling a shallow silver dish with a mixture of some sort combining the ingredients of three of the bottles on the smaller table, handed the dish to Maartens who in turn placed it carefully on the breast of the corpse. The old woman had long since stopped her babbling, leaning her head back and closing her eyes in manifest exhaustion. Maartens and Devereaux closed in on the body from either side, each with stethoscope in hand, Devereaux placing his under the left ear, Maartens his under the heart. Devereaux straightened almost at once, his face emotionless, but Maartens continued to listen to the heart. Minutes passed in silence until at length Maartens called Devereaux to his side and whispered to him. Devereaux nodded, placing his instrument on the heart as Maartens hastily removed his own.

"Mirror!"

Standing behind Maartens, the nurse searched among the bottles and instruments and finding a small hand mirror gave it to him, and he held it over the dead girl's mouth. Devereaux said something intelligible only to Maartens. The silver dish containing the concoction was removed and Maartens changed the angle of the glass.

"Wine," he snapped. Nurse Raphael ran out of the room, returning with a glass half-filled with red wine. By now the couple watching had gotten up from their chairs and were moving up the table to the head of the casket. "Sit down!" ordered Maartens irritably.

"But, doctor . . ." began the man.

"Do as I tell you, please! We've reached an extremely critical point. If anything goes wrong now you'll have only yourselves to blame. Take your seats!"

Father and mother exchanged glances and returned to their chairs, vanishing from Alison's view.

"Epinephrine!" exclaimed Maartens.

The nurse put the wine down, handing him instead a small vial of light brown liquid. Then she began bringing the shorter candles up to the head of the long table, arranging them in a semicircle framing the face of the dead girl in their flickering light. Maartens put the open end of the vial to the girl's nostrils, first one, then the other, with one hand while continuing to hold the mirror in position at her mouth with the other.

"Yes! Yes!" Devereaux was nodding vigorously, his face breaking into a look of triumph. Approaching the small table, he picked up the wine, holding it in readiness at Maartens' left elbow. Maartens himself lifted the mirror, displaying it to the man and woman.

"She is breathing!"

"Dear God be praised!" screamed the woman.

Maartens removed the vial, took the wine from Devereaux and gently and carefully moistened the girl's lips with it. Then he handed the vial to the nurse.

"Otto."

Nurse Raphael went to get Otto, who appeared almost immediately. Following Maartens' gesture, he shuffled to the table, standing by as the two doctors lifted the girl out of the casket. Otto then picked the casket up as easily as if it had been papier mache and carried it out of the room while the girl was carefully placed on the table, Nurse Raphael slipping a pillow beneath her head.

Slowly, the lids drawn upward by invisible threads, the eyes opened, scanning the ceiling, and closed. And the chest rose as her lungs took in air. Maartens gave her the wine, administering it in sips, and Devereaux resumed listening to her heart with his stethoscope. Her eyes opened and stayed open and her breathing adjusted to a normal rhythm. Chairs scraped the floor and the father and mother came forward, the mother covering her daughter's forehead with kisses while the father gently stroked her right hand.

And ignored by all the others present, Maartens' mother, awakening from her sleep, lifted her face, saw what had happened and, smiling broadly, slowly nodded approval.

4

Too tired to fall asleep at once, too overwhelmed and unnerved by what she had seen, Alison lay in her bed pondering the whole sequence of events culminating in the revival of the dead girl. Again she was forced to admit that she had underestimated Dr. Maartens. Still, his incredible success, admirable though it may have been, only served to intensify her uneasiness and her abhorrence and mistrust of Barringer House and of those who occupied it.

How she longed for home, for her mother, her poor unfortunate father and for Charles, with his extraordinary laugh. For Gene Hampton as well. Strange how much she missed the man with the flaming hair, having only met him. Such an unfortunately brief time for a budding friendship now that she thought about it. She could only hope that their paths would cross again, although at the moment such a possibility seemed discouragingly remote. She fancied Gene and Charles suddenly appearing, riding up to the front door on snorting stallions, dashing up the stairs and into her room and escorting her out of the house, whisking her miles away, out of sight of Maartens and Devereaux and the whole alien crew of them!

Second thoughts crept into her mind, over her eagerness to witness the proceedings of the night. She had planned to watch no more than an hour or so, but it had been nearly three hours before Maartens was able to bring the dead girl back to life. And once she, herself, had started watching there was, of course, no stopping, with the result that she was far too weary to even consider leaving that night. Besides, even before she had replaced the chair, locked the door behind her and returned to lock herself in her own room, rain had come rolling in from the sea, whipping against the windowpanes and leveling the surface of the water below. It was heavy, but it gave no threat of attaining anything like the violence of the previous downpour, and yet it would once again mire the roads and if she chose to leave could soak her to the skin over the distance she would have to walk to reach the nearest town. Surely by morning or noon hour at the latest it would let up and hopefully the following night would be clear and more favorable.

She slept until late morning, awakening to find her breakfast tray, with cold eggs, soggy toast and tepid tea, perched on the nightstand. Nurse Raphael came into the room while she was downing her toast and introduced herself. She was tall, angular, with puffy eyes and a prominent nose as red as a sot's at the tip, lending her an almost ludicrous appearance. She wore her dark-brown hair tightly bound in a knot at the back of her head and her eyes and tone betrayed a peevish mood, as if Maartens or Devereaux had ordered her upstairs to the room against her wishes and having arrived she couldn't wait to deliver her speech and be gone.

"Dr. Maartens is busy all day and won't be able to see you."

"He wouldn't be avoiding me . . ."

"Try discussing that with him when you do see him." She yawned and covered her mouth with two fingers. Alison suppressed a smile. While the general slept after his victory, the troops were obliged to arise as usual and see to his obligations along with their own. "You haven't eaten your breakfast."

"It's cold."

"Pity. You might have waked up at a decent hour. I should think you'd get enough sleep lying in bed all day. Which reminds me, your door will be left unlocked until bedtime."

"Why lock it then? What if there's a fire? Way up here I'd be helpless as a baby."

Nurse Raphael made a face which Alison judged to be the closest thing to a smile she was capable of.

"You don't look like the helpless sort to me. And oh yes, Dr. Maartens wishes you to take your meals downstairs from now on, with Alma and Otto in the kitchen. We've more to do here than wait on the likes of you hand and foot."

"I'm sure of that."

"Beginning with lunch."

"You don't really expect me to eat with Otto . . ."

"You'll eat with Otto or not at all, whatever you choose."

"I'd like to speak with Dr. Maartens."

"Not today, he's not available."

"Is he sleeping?"

The nurse frowned and shook her head. "He's busy, he can't be disturbed."

"I insist!"

"Insist all you like." Nurse Raphael took the tray and went to the door. "Lunch is at twelve o'clock in the kitchen, with Alma and Otto."

Alma came for her a few minutes before twelve. "So you're staying with us I see. Isn't that nice."

"Is it?"

"Come along. There's chicken soup and a bit of ham for your highness."

"You'll have to wait till I get dressed."

"I'll wait, hurry it up."

Alma sat on the bed singing to herself as Alison put on her dress and shoes and moments later followed the older woman downstairs to the main floor. She was tempted to question her about the layout of the house, but having no real desire for conversation of any sort, refrained from doing so. On the way to the kitchen, they passed through the living room and above the fireplace was a portrait of a wild-eyed, dark-haired girl barely twenty years old. She wore a tight-fitting crimson gown and a gold necklace and large hoop earrings. Directly across from her hung a rather good oil painting of a bearded middle-aged man in the uniform of a sea captain, Captain Barringer no doubt. His hard blue eyes stared across the room at the girl, betraying a gleam that combined fascination and Puritanical disapproval in equal measure. Perhaps the lady from Portugal wouldn't smile quite so mischievously, nor toss her pretty head so wantonly, if she had known that fate would one day find her carved up and fed to the ancestors of the sharks presently prowling the waters at the base of the cliff.

The living room was cluttered with heavy wooden and leather furniture, with nothing resembling a woman's touch. A cumbersome divan with room for four was drawn up before the fireplace, its back to a table with an elaborately carved but homely border. Stretched down the length of the table was a richly embroidered linen cloth in gold and white, and upon the cloth stood a vase filled with dried marigolds and mums. The walls were paneled and along with the paintings of Captain Barringer and his ill-fated friend, a coat of arms, ostensibly that of the Barringers, a small harpoon and an excellent seascape were hung.

The entrance to the dining room was distinguished by a

modified ogee arch fashioned like so much else in the house of oak. In contrast, the kitchen was surprisingly bright and cheerful and quite large, even for a house that size. Copper cookware was neatly hung from hooks attached to a metal frame suspended from the center of the ceiling, the floor was stone skillfully pieced together without mortar by some long dead area artisan, and a black monster stove concealed most of the far wall opposite the sinks.

A well-scrubbed table occupied the space under the window, and a smaller table was located by the entrance. One side was against the wall and three stools stood at the other three sides. Two stools only were visible, however, Otto occupying the third, his elbows planted firmly on the table, his face halfway down into his soup, his spoon directing it to his mouth where it was drawn up with a loud slurping sound that for Alison promised to set a mood of rare delicacy and breeding for her forthcoming meal.

Happily, throughout the entire meal, Otto never looked up from his plate, finishing his soup and holding his spoon out of the way so that Alma had room to refill the bowl using a wooden dipper. Occasionally, his hands went to the loaf of homemade bread on a plate in the center of the table and tearing loose one fistful after another he would plunge them into the soup and cram them into his mouth.

Alison ate in silence, dissuaded from looking at him by the melodious sounds rising from his spoon as it came in contact with his mouth. Finishing eating, she asked Alma politely if she might tour the house, but the response was a firm refusal and there seemed little to be gained by pressing the point, since it was likely that the order had come down from the miracle worker himself.

The miracle worker. How had the great Dr. Maartens brought it off? How was he able to take a corpse with all bodily functions stopped, no heartbeat, no blood flow, no muscle movement, no sign of life whatsoever, prepared by a mortician and placed in a casket, and literally breathe life back into it? The process from beginning to end was complicated, extremely involved, three hours of unceasing effort, one procedure after another preceded and accompanied by the old woman's chanting, until she collapsed in exhaustion. What bearing had her babbling on the turnabout? Was it all purely window dressing, tinsel and colored streamers for the onlookers? Or were the purpled candles, the robes, the strange language truly a part of it, even the key to its success?

Pragmatist that she was, she couldn't believe that the old woman's contribution had anything to do with bringing the girl back to life, any more than if she'd read tarot cards over her or trilled on a flute. But then, if anyone had told her that such an astonishing resuscitation had been effected at all, spiritually, medically or otherwise, she wouldn't have believed it.

She idled away the afternoon in her room, with the door unlocked. The rain stopped about one o'clock and the sun came out, but the air was chilly and the sea looked wintry, the tops of the waves ripping off, white lace showing itself on first one then another, like shapeless beds of white flowers springing en masse from fertile earth. She would have liked to return to the library up the corridor and browse through Dr. Devereaux's books, but she wasn't supposed to know about that room or anything in it, least of all the newspaper clipping.

Perhaps now that she thought about it it might be wise to take that paper along with her. If no one in Harwich or Brunswick or Philadelphia believed her lurid tale, at least the Albany police might show some interest. But again, getting out and away from Barringer House took first priority, and anything that might further delay her departure was worth neither time nor consideration.

She decided to leave on the stroke of midnight, for no other reason but that the witching hour seemed ideally suited to her situation. Hopefully the blue-white clouds stretched out now and no longer bellied gray with rain would break away from each other and wander off to another sky to allow the moon to show itself and light her way. If it began raining again, she could not let that stop her. She had already been too long in Barringer House, the urge to escape was beginning to possess her, like some vengeful spirit, and her desire to get free of Maartens and the rest of them was becoming an obsession. It was as if the house itself was no longer a tangible structure of wood and stone, but rather some loathsome pestilence infecting her mind and body.

She could take solace in the assurance that Maartens apparently had no intention of harming her. She may have been an inconvenience, even an annoyance, but she was no real threat. Still, he obviously did not know what to do with her. As things stood, he couldn't possibly let her walk out the door. She could thank her stars for one thing, however: that he didn't suspect that she had witnessed the entire exhibition. Had he known that, he probably would have had Otto throw her out the window into the sea!

But there it was, the wall between them complicating everything and rendering solution impossible. He knew that she had seen enough the night before last to arouse her suspicions; so there was no way he could trust her out of the house.

A half hour after the sun went away, Nurse Raphael came by to tell her that she was invited to dinner in the dining room at eight o'clock.

"Wine in the living room at seven-thirty."

"How very hospitable of you."

"You seem to have no trouble forgetting that you're an uninvited guest in this house."

"One who'd prefer to be on her way. Far be it from me to inconvenience anyone. You know, Miss . . ."

"Mrs."

"Mrs. Raphael, your Dr. Maartens' holding me here against my will is kidnapping. He can go to prison for twenty years, and he will. But not alone. You and everyone else in this house is just as responsible. You can be put away for as long as he'll be."

"Is that supposed to frighten me?"

"Not at all, it's just something you ought to think about. On the other hand, if you help me get word to my cousin Charles, Dr. Charles Collier in Harwich, your complicity would end immediately. You wouldn't even go to trial, much less prison."

"My, we're well versed in the law, aren't we?"

"Will you help me?"

"Seven-thirty in the living room, and don't be late. I understand dinner will be roast venison."

She left. Damn the woman! She'd go running straight to Maartens. Then again, maybe she wouldn't. That sort of offer was to be expected, why bother reporting it to him? She'd get no medal for passing the test of loyalty.

For the dozenth time in the past few hours, Alison reflected on her situation. She had passed four days in Barringer House, four days that seemed more like four months. If she tried to get out that night and failed, if Otto or Devereaux or Maartens himself caught her and brought her back, what then? What would they do, chain her to her bed? How long would they hold her, weeks, months? Probably until they moved on, whenever that might be. The incident involving Maartens and the Lyons girl in Albany had sent them running out of town. If Maartens was still on the run, if Barringer House was only a stopover, a hideout until the police picked up his trail again, they could all of them be leaving soon. The fact that Devereaux hadn't bothered to unpack all his books lent further substance to this assumption, and yet what made her think that even if they did leave they'd let her go? More likely they'd pack her up along with the books. It was a little like being kidnapped by gypsies.

In the musty-smelling living room a fire blazed in the fireplace, the flames guarded by two dour-looking lions crouched atop their andirons. Dr. Maartens was in an ebullient mood, his pale features wreathed in a broad smile. Obviously he was still savoring his triumph of the previous night. Where the dead girl brought to life was now, at home in bed or up and around, there was no way of determining, of course, but it was clear from the doctor's behavior that the victory he'd gained was a permanent one, at least in his opinion.

"Ah, Miss Collier, what a delightful surprise. And what a welcome addition to our table. A new face among all the old ones, eh?"

He raised his wine in salute and motioned her to the divan. Then he seized the poker and stoked the fire, sending a shower of snapping sparks climbing up the chimney. No sooner had she sat down than Alma materialized at her elbow, as sour-faced as ever and holding a silver tray with two glasses of wine on it.

"Either one."

"A quite exceptional sauterne," said Maartens. "Captain

Barringer kept a superb cellar. The man was a true connoisseur. Seafaring men generally have such limited tastes in food and drink, a tot of rum, gin, ale . . . but Barringer was different. Exceptional taste, outstanding." He raised his glass to the portrait of the Portuguese girl and then to Captain Barringer's opposite it and, having made his little joke, took his seat in a high-backed chair at right angles to the fire. Nurse Raphael sat in the matching chair on the other side of the fire, but although present in body, her eyes indicated her mind was miles away. She was, Alison assumed, in attendance by imperial command. Alison tasted the wine. It was bitter, but then all wine was bitter to her; she rarely drank, having no taste for wine or liquor of any sort.

"Very good," she said.

"Bouquet, full, generous. Don't you agree, Constance?"

Nurse Raphael nodded and sipped.

"I understand we're to have venison," said Alison "it sounds delicious."

"You've never tasted it?"

"No."

"Tsk tsk, neglect of palate." Maartens waggled his finger. "You'll find it delightful, especially the way Alma prepares it. Gamy, but mouth watering. But don't eat too much. It has been known to bully the digestion. There'll be little onions, too, boiled, hardly larger than pearls, and fresh carrots and surprises. Alma always keeps one or two surprises for us, don't you, Alma?"

Alma grunted unenthusiastically and walked off with her tray, leaving the odd glass of sauterne on the table behind the divan.

"Will Dr. Devereaux be joining us?" asked Alison.

"Oh my, yes," said Maartens. He finished his wine and started on the glass left on the table, pausing to consult his watch. "He'll be down any minute now. Well, Miss Collier, tell me what do you think of this marvelous old house?"

"What I've seen of it is very impressive."

"You must see all of it. First thing tomorrow, I myself will take you on a tour. We mustn't neglect our guests."

"Guests?"

"Oh yes, people are continually dropping in on us. You're not drinking your wine. Doesn't the taste appeal to you?"

"It's fine, thank you."

Taking a deep breath, she drank a third of the glass, instantly regretted it, and held her breath until the fire went out in her throat.

"If you'd like something else . . ."

"No, no . . ."

"This house, one can easily read the character of Captain Barringer from the way he had it built, and the manner in which he furnished it. There are so many clues. Simple deductive reasoning. A connoisseur of fine wines and a reader of good books, therefore an intelligent man. But a dreamer." Maartens indicated the girl's picture over the fireplace. "His lady friend was less than half his age when he took up with her. Foolish, foolish man."

"What is so foolish about falling in love?" asked Nurse Raphael coldly. The statement was so unexpected and so frank in tone, Alison was more amused than startled by it.

"A man in his fifties falling in love with a girl barely twenty? A fiery little minx like that . . ."

"But who is to say they didn't love each other?"

"He murdered her, didn't he? In cold blood, brutally."

"What has that to do with it?"

"I put it to you, Miss Collier. Can a slip of a child of twenty love a man in his fifties?"

"It's happened," said Alison, glancing at Nurse Raphael for approval and getting it, the ends of the woman's mouth rising slightly.

"You women, two starry-eyed romantics, that's what you are!" He laughed and slapped his knee. "Something else I've discovered about our bearded friend, he wasn't satisfied with life, not by a long shot."

"Who is?" asked Nurse Raphael.

"In the dining room you'll see . . . Excuse me, I am. Yes, I am! As I was saying, in the dining room you'll see dozens of paintings, most of them whaling scenes. And yet Barringer never commanded a whaler in his entire life. He transported teak and tapioca, rum and pitch and cotton, everything, but he never chased a whale as much as half a league."

"You're sure of that?" Alison took another sip of her wine, aware that at the rate she was going there would still be some in her glass the following noon.

"His diary is upstairs. I'll show it to you after dinner if you're interested. Fascinating reading. A dreamer, yes, and as superstitious as the greenest cabin boy. Now, there's an interesting subject, superstitions of the sea."

Nurse Raphael suppressed a yawn, silent disagreement. But Maartens was not to be stopped.

"All seamen, from Laplanders to Chinese, are superstitious, particularly about the moon. Sign of weather, you know. If the moon's horns look sharp, the weather will be good, but when the new moon lies on her back, her horns up, beware. On occasion, the dark side of the moon is visible, the part of the moon in shadow can be seen through it. The new moon carrying the old moon in her arms says the sailor. Sure sign of rough weather. A misty circle surrounding the moon presages rain, the distance of the circle from the moon indicating the time of its arrival, shortly for close in, a longer period for further out. Am I boring you, also?"

"I'd better ask Alma to go up and get John," said Nurse Raphael.

Maartens looked at his watch again. At that moment, Alma appeared in the archway leading to the dining room.

"Dinner's long since ready. The meat'll be overcooked," she announced petulantly. "Oh, there you are," she added, looking past the group.

Dr. Devereaux had come in, his long blond hair tousled over his forehead, eyes bleary, his hand finding the back of Nurse Raphael's chair to steady himself. He had been drinking, and conscious of how much, he made an effort to improve his posture and effect an impression which might be mistaken for sobriety.

"Sorry I'm late, unavoidable detained." His inability to get out the "ly" sent his eyebrows upward self-consciously. But he managed a friendly nod of greeting to Maartens and Nurse Raphael in turn, before pausing at Alison and staring.

"John," said Dr. Maartens, "let me introduce Miss Alison Collier of Philadelphia."

"Pleasure, Miss Alison Collier Philadelphia."

"You can all come in now," interjected Alma.

They filed into the dining room to a table set with a lovely lace cloth, silver and dinnerware neatly arranged, and a bowl heaped with pine cones, dried corn and gourds shellacked and shining serving as a centerpiece. Above the table hung a ship's wheel converted into a chandelier. The walls of the room seen only fleetingly by Alison on her way through earlier in the day boasted a number of paintings, the majority whaling scenes as Dr. Maartens had said.

She was seated opposite Maartens, her back to the

double doors which, when she examined the floor plan of the house in her mind, must open upon the large room visible from the railing upstairs. Nurse Raphael sat across from Devereaux, casting admiring glances his way. He smelled strongly of rum, as if he'd not only been drinking it, but using it for shaving lotion as well. He was good-looking in a disheveled and neglected way, his jacket collar awry, his hair hastily combed and a small piece of court plaster high on his left cheek where he'd evidently cut himself shaving. Maartens looked at him disapprovingly but without comment, seemingly determined not to let either Devereaux's tardiness nor his appearance affect his own good humor. Tasting his victory, the doctor was like a small boy who'd landed the big fish, dying to brag about it, but unable to, satisfied to bubble over with hail-fellow-well-met conversation, his every word a musical note.

"We were talking about superstitions of the sea," he said to Devereaux.

"How nice," said the younger man, grinning at Alison, "may I have the bloody butter, please?"

She obliged, passing the dish, and he carved a great gob of it onto his bread and butter plate, reaching for the bread. Alma brought in the first course, a molded fruit salad that looked delicious.

Dr. Devereaux had no desire to talk about superstitions of any sort.

"Small talk, what bloody good is it? There's too much that's important to talk about to waste breath over small talk. Agree, Miss Alison Collier of Philadelphia?"

She smiled and shrugged, aware that whether she agreed or not he was prepared to plunge ahead.

"Then we'll talk about whatever you like, John," said Maartens.

"John, you've cut yourself," said Nurse Raphael, giving Devereaux a look that showed unmistakably that her detached attitude toward him in his absence while the three of them waited in the living room had been only a cover for her true feelings.

"Razor cut me, Constance love, I had nothing to do with it."

Maartens laughed and Devereaux looked bored.

"Want me to take a look at it?" asked the nurse.

"Please, Constance, eat your bloody fruit smash or whatever it is!"

Nurse Raphael pouted, hurt to the quick, her eyes darting first to Maartens, then to Alison, and back down to her food.

"Small talk is nothing but a design on a Japanese screen," observed Devereaux.

"I don't follow you, John." Maartens paused between forkfuls of his fruit.

"Japanese screen, the screen we all put up to block other people's view of us. You'd think we were all bloody naked! Bunch of frauds, that's what people are, every bloody one of us. Except you, Miss Alison Collier. I don't know you well enough to judge. But me, I'm a fraud, total . . . biggest fraud in the world. King of the frauds, that's me, *Doctor* Devereaux." He laughed bitterly, shaking his head. "Miss Alison Collier, what would you say if I told you that I'm no more a doctor than you are?"

"John, I say we should change the subject," said Maartens patiently. "There are so many pleasant things to talk about. What are you reading now?"

"See!" snapped the other man. "There you have it, Japanese screen. Cover reality with sugar. Miss Alison Collier, you are looking at a man who was once a fairly distinguished physician. Not a great one, not even a very good one, perhaps, but a physician nonetheless, degree and license to practice and all. Hippocratic Oath. You familiar with the Hippocratic Oath? Course not." He raised his right hand solemnly. "The regimen I adopt shall be for the benefit of my patients according to my duty and judgment, and not for their hurt or for any wrong. I will give no deadly drug to any, though it be asked of me, nor will I counsel such, and especially I will not aid a woman to procure abortion. Whatsoever house I enter, there will I go for the benefit of the sick, refraining from all wrong-doing or corruption. Amazing, rules of the game. Broken 'em all, and more, and so my fellow distinguished physicians have chucked me out of the bloody fraternity, taken the scalpel to the M.D. after my bloody name and removed it, cleanly, no infection, no complications. Not much!"

"John, John, why do you torture yourself so?" shrilled Nurse Raphael.

"Torture? You see, Miss Alison Collier, just as I tell you, all sham and fraud! Here I bare my bloody soul, I speak the absolute unvarnished truth, story of my life, and I'm accused of torturing myself! No, Constance, no, no, no, cover it up, hide it all under a blanket of lies, that's torture, that hurts in here." He tapped his breast with his fist. "No, why should I live a lie? Why should any man? Because you do? Here, Miss Collier, we have another sterling example of the Japanese screen up and hiding the real person. Isn't that so, Constance? Isn't it?"

"Enough," said Maartens, "kindly eat your dinner. It's delicious."

"Nurse Raphael, *Mrs.* Raphael. I'll wager you can't guess who Mr. Raphael was, can you, Miss Collier? Don't try, because he's long gone. Bloody Fiji Islands, Ultima Thule . . ."

"That's a filthy lie. My husband died and you know it!"

"Died? The hell he did. He ran away, and *you* know it! You told me so yourself in your bloody cups. Couldn't get his arms around to hold his ministering angel, her wings in the bloody way! Imagine a man making love to a pillar of salt? Ha! Nurse Raphael. Real name Rayfield. Common name, too bloody common. Had to change it to Italian painter. Ever see such incredible vanity in your life?"

"STOP IT!" Maartens' hand came down hard on the table, his silverware jumping in place, and he rose to his feet glowering at Devereaux. "No more of this!"

Enough for the doctor, it was evidently more than enough for Nurse Raphael, who was on her feet also, pushing her chair back and bursting into tears. Maartens reached for her arm, but avoiding him, she ran out of the room and up the stairs.

"Constance . . . you forgot your screen!" Devereaux was suddenly embarrassed, sobered by the unexpected consequence of his boorish behavior while Maartens glared at him, his rage rising.

"You damned fool!"

"Easy, Louis . . ."

"Drunken boor!"

"No you don't, don't start with me . . ."

"Why I put up with you heaven only knows!"

"That's funny, that's bloody hilarious that is! We both know why you put up with me! And if only heaven knows the mud we've been up to our elbows in these three bloody years we're the luckiest pigs in the barnyard!"

"Go to your room!"

Devereaux looked at Alison and grinned impishly. "I'm a bad boy. Bad boys go to their rooms and stand in the bloody corner. And no supper . . ."

"Alma will bring it up to you. You have ten seconds to leave this table!"

Devereaux drew himself up to his full height, saluted Maartens smartly and marched away. Alma appeared holding the tray with the venison, her apron protecting her hands from the heat.

"What's the matter?"

"Nothing, Alma." Maartens was suddenly subdued and coloring slightly. Still on his feet, he looked embarrassingly at Alison. "Forgive this disgraceful exhibition. He drinks too much. He can't handle it, never could. Please eat your dinner, I shall be down in a minute. I must see to Con . . . Nurse Raphael."

He left.

Alison took a portion of the venison and began eating. It was indeed gamy, but delicious. Her eyes wandered to the paintings before her. One frame was missing, she mused, the one surrounding "God bless our happy home."

Doctor John Devereaux and Nurse Constance Raphael, theirs was something less than a mutual affection. Devereaux had painted a remarkably clear picture of the two of them. A pity he hadn't gotten round to Dr. Maartens, but then of course Maartens would never have permitted that. Besides, all she needed to know about the miracle worker she knew already, enough to convince her that nothing must stand in the way of her leaving that night. No more delays. Twelve o'clock and out the door, out the window, out!

She could hear the nurse screaming and sobbing, her voice drifting down the stairs, through the living room, through the archway to where she sat eating. Happily, her appetite was unaffected by the incident. Maartens was upstairs trying to calm down the nurse, but with little success. Alison took a second helping of venison, drenching it with gravy, thinking hopefully as she did that perhaps the deer would help her run like a deer.

She would have to sacrifice one of her bags, the two would load her down. She chose the reticule in preference to the valise.

Maartens returned, but without either Nurse Raphael or Devereaux, the two of them sulking in their rooms leaving empty chairs at the table and all the more dinner for her.

"Again, I apologize."

"There's no need to, Dr. Maartens. These things happen in the best of families."

He did not smile. The incident had upset him, not alone disrupting his happy frame of mind, but depleting as well the self-satisfaction he nurtured knowing that he was the general of the group and in complete command. Command of a drunken boor and a deluded and thoroughly miserable neurotic.

He invited her to have coffee and brandy in the living room with him, and she accepted the one, politely declining the other.

"It's a rather good cognac," he said, holding his glass at eye level and peering through it at the fire. "It's sure to help you sleep."

"I have no difficulty sleeping, doctor."

"You're a remarkable young woman, Miss Collier."

"What on earth makes you say that?"

"I mean it. You take adversity in stride like a trouper. Like my dear mother, rest her soul."

Interesting, she thought, another lie to add to his earlier ones.

"I don't consider this adversity," she said evenly. "The problem is yours, not mine. You have a very important decision to make. What precisely do you do with your uninvited guest?"

"You make it sound as if you were a rose bush or a basket of apples, something I can't find a place for. I see no problem, you will continue on as our guest."

"Until . . ."

"Until we move on."

"And when might that be?"

"Who can say? When our work is done. Not long."

"I don't suppose there's any possibility of your letting me contact my mother. As I told you, she's laid up in bed . . ."

"And worried about you, of course. I have a thought. Why not write her a note, nothing too informative, just a few words to tell her you're perfectly safe, that no harm has come to you and that you'll be home in a few weeks."

"Weeks?"

"Well, perhaps it's best not to touch on the time. Tell you what, you write the note, give it to me and I'll see that Otto posts it in Brunswick next time he goes to town."

"The way Dr. Devereaux contacted my cousin?"

Maartens made a gesture of helplessness. "That's not fair. How could we contact your cousin? He'd come running up here binging who knows who or what with him. This, a note to your mother, is a different matter entirely. Write it. You have my word as a gentleman that it will be posted. I'll have Alma bring stationery and a pen and ink to your room, if you like."

"Thank you."

Neither the nurse nor Dr. Devereaux came back downstairs, although the former calmed down and the latter could be heard snoring lustily as Alison bid Dr. Maartens good night and, taking a candle, mounted the stairs, having first declined his invitation to spend a few minutes looking through Captain Barringer's diary.

No sooner had she reached her room than Alma arrived with stationery and writing utensils.

"Did you like the venison?"

"It was delicious, Alma."

That pleased her, the stubborn mouth relaxing, the eyes brightening, and she said good night and left.

Minutes later, Alison heard the door being locked from the outside and Otto's distinctive shuffle fading down the corridor. It was a quarter to eleven by her watch.

Transferring a few things from her mother's bag to her own, she placed the reticule at the foot of the bed and sat down at the table to write:

Dear Dr. Maartens,

I have enjoyed my visit with you here at Barringer House immensely. The house itself is most impressive and the company ideal.

Should you ever come to Philadelphia, I shall be very disappointed if you do not come to visit me and allow me the opportunity to reciprocate.

I repeat, your home is marvelous and your associates among the most fascinating people I have ever been privileged to meet.

Thank you again for your hospitality.

Very truly yours,
(Miss) Eleanor Lyons

Blowing the ink dry, she folded the note, placing it in the envelope, then, folding the flap inside, wrote a single line across the envelope:

"Doctor Louis Moore or
Doctor Hendrik Maartens"

At midnight, she picked up her bag and fastening the clasp of her cloak under her chin, unlocked the door and went outside, locking it behind her. The house was asleep, the only sound Devereaux's muffled snoring coming from down the corridor.

Moving down to the large door, she let herself through it and paused at the railing for a last look at the room below. A single candle burned by the door at the left and as she watched, Otto came in and snuffed it out. At the sight of him, she backed against the wall and held her breath, but he went out of the room again without so much as a backward glance.

Reaching the top of the stairs, she started down, past the diagonal line of portraits of nameless seafaring Barringers leading down to the foyer. Now she was within twenty feet of the front door. So far it had been easier than she could have hoped for. The activities of the night before having exhausted the performers, they slept soundly, with the exception of Otto who seemed to survive without ever putting his head down on a pillow. Pausing, she could hear sounds coming from far over on the other side of the house near the kitchen, Otto or Alma probably cleaning up the last of the dinner dishes.

She approached the door stealthily to keep her heels from clicking against the stone floor. The door was locked and bolted, but the bolt slid across easily and the key in the lock turned with hardly a sound. Slowly she opened the door and the night breeze gently touched her face, caressing her cheek, the darkness welcoming her appearance. She closed the door quietly behind her and, gripping her bag, straightened her back proudly and started down the winding gravel path. The gate ahead was obscured by tall hedges still clinging to their green leaves while all about them the trees continued to yield their foliage to the frost and the wind.

There was a chill in the air, the wind hard at work and the all but leafless trees rising above the hedges bent slowly back and forth, scratching the starless sky with the tips of their branches. Looking back, she could see the house in total darkness. Leaving it, shedding it like a chrysalis, filled her with exhilaration—the sudden sensation of absolute freedom, and the musty odor of the dark and gloomy rooms no longer in her nostrils, replaced by clean, sweet-smelling sea air.

She walked down the way to the coach circle that, she presumed, started and ended at the main gate. The gate itself loomed before her, a great iron wall joining the walls of stone on either side.

Her heart began pounding. What if it were locked? Dear Lord, it couldn't be! But it must be, people always locked their gates at night, particularly people like Dr. Maartens with so many secrets to conceal from the outside world. Dropping her bag, she clutched her skirt with both hands and ran toward the gate. Reaching it, grasping in the blackness of its shadow, her fingers found the twin rings, twisting first one, then the other.

Locked! And as if she needed more proof of its condition she could make out the heavy metal supports midway up it, one on either side holding a ponderous wooden beam in place.

There would be no leaving Barringer House by this gate. If only it weren't so solid, if only it were vertical bars with horizontal supports, at least she might climb it! But no such luck. Walking back to where she had dropped her bag, she brought it with her and began looking over the wall foot by foot, beginning at the left of the gate and moving slowly along to the corner. Reaching it, she started back down toward the house, looking frantically for a ladder, a trellis, a small tree, anything she might climb to reach the top.

The wall stood nearly fifteen feet high, but might just as well have been ten times that for all the luck she was having finding a way over it. Rhododendrons and evergreens lined the inside of it, none taller than three feet.

The magnitude of her plight became progressively clearer as she moved down the wall from the corner in the direction of the house. Even had she been able to reach the top of the wall, how could she possibly descend the other side without breaking an ankle or worse?

Then one more problem presented itself; unlike the majority of large homes bounded by walls, Barringer House had no need for complete encirclement, the rear being perched at the summit of the cliff overlooking the sea. So the wall came to an abrupt end at the right front corner of the house, joining it.

The wall at the left began at the left corner and was built straight out to join the gate wall.

It took only a few minutes to inspect the full length completely. There was, she decided, a way up it for a fly or a spider, perhaps, but not for a young woman burdened with a fairly heavy bag and with little experience in climbing anything more difficult than a flight of stairs.

She was tempted to sit down and have a good cry. It was overdue. Her nerves would have appreciated that, tangled as they were, knotted and taut. But she was too angry to give in to tears.

Neither wishing nor praying would transport her to the other side and freedom and there was obviously no way up the thing, nor even, for that matter, up the side of the house at either corner from where she might step over to the top of the wall.

She wondered fleetingly if Maartens had planned it all. If he really did admire her strength in the face of adversity, perhaps he also thought her resourceful. Maybe he took it for granted that one way or another she would escape her locked bedroom. It would please him no end knowing that once she made it through the front door there was no possible way to get out of the grounds.

So she was beaten. But was she? Was anyone really defeated until they conceded defeat, until they willingly surrendered?

A thought crossed her mind, a wild, quixotic, absurd and dangerous idea. An inspiration grounded on the perfectly practical premise that every house with a front door has a back door. And if a house had no back door, why then one took the bull by the horns and made one!

But deciding to alter her strategy was not nearly the same as implementing that strategy. For suddenly a fresh obstacle appeared. Returning to the front door, she tried it only to find that during her brief tour of the grounds, Otto or someone else inside had locked up for the night a second time.

What luck! Adversity piling on misfortune! The door was locked, so the inside bolt had to be thrown as well.

But she had to get back into the house. To be found outside in the morning would be bad enough, but when Maartens or anyone else found the envelope addressed with the doctor's two names and read her note she would be in much deeper trouble than she was already.

What a fool she had been, what a childish thing to do!

Moving to the left of the door, she examined the nearest window. It was locked, as were all five windows, including the oriel which upon examination seemed the least promising way into the house. Through each of the smaller windows, the casement catch could be vaguely seen within inches of the glass. Finding a stone, she wrapped the hem of her cloak around it and shattered the small lozenge-shaped pane framing the catch of the window nearest the front door. The sound of the glass breaking was like a cannon going off, but after holding her breath for what seemed fully five minutes, she concluded that nobody inside had been awakened by the sound, and picking away the fragments of broken glass, she reached through and unlocked the window. Raising it slowly, she lifted her reticule through it, climbing in after it and closing the window.

Dr. Devereaux was still snoring lustily as she passed by his room, reached her own and unlocked the door with her makeshift tool. Once inside, she crumpled the note to Maartens and, opening the window, dropped it into the water.

She looked at her watch. Only twenty-five minutes had passed in her futile attempt at escape. The moon hung over the sea, the solitary witness to her failure, its light revealing the surface below. The water was calmer than she had ever seen it. No whitecaps tousled the waves, the waves themselves barely visible.

Leaning far out the window and looking straight down, she estimated the distance to the water as eighty or ninety feet. Should she attempt it?

Pulling down the drape ropes, she tied all four of them together, judging their length when joined at about fifty feet. Then she pulled both sheets off the bed and laying them one atop the other on the floor decided that they would add about eighteen feet at most. Not enough. She would have to rip them in two and pray that her weight would not pull them apart.

Breaking a pane of glass, she took one of the shards to

cut the top seams of both sheets and quickly tore them into even halves. These she added one by one to the rope.

Now, where should she tie the end of the thing? The window frames were wood and severely weathered on the outside, cracked and dry, and her weight on the rope could easily snap them. She decided to tie the top end around the leg of the bed, which made it necessary to move the bed over to the window so as not to lose precious rope length and to avoid starting down and dragging the bed loudly across the bare floor with her weight.

Inch by inch she moved the bed quietly toward the window. She then fastened the end of the rope around the leg and, leaning out the window a second time, looked straight down.

This was the worst part of it, worse than the actual descent. She had only Alma's word for what lay at the base of the cliff. And even that was secondhand information. Before the two of them had had their falling out, Alma had mentioned a cave at the bottom.

"There's a secret stairway that goes down from the cellar to the landing. Small boats were able to go into the cave and tie up underneath."

If smugglers brought their loot in there to hide it in the house, there had to be a dock and, God willing, a small boat! Or was that too much to hope for?

Looking at the black side, if there were no boat, if there were nothing to carry her out of the cave into open water, up the shore a reasonable distance where she could land and begin looking for a sign to Harwich, she would have no choice but to swim along the base of the cliff.

The night air was cold, the water would be freezing. She could swim, she would have to. Unfortunately, she was not an excellent swimmer, not like Grace Swann, the little blond fish. And she wouldn't get twenty feet up the way floundering about in her dress and cloak.

But entering the water in her underclothing only, she could catch pneumonia. That was a chance she would have to take. Removing her dress, she bundled it around her shoes, wrapping her cloak around the bundle and tying it firmly to the other end of her rope. Then she let it down to a point a few feet above the surface.

She would descend to just above the bundle. With any luck at all, there would be moonlight enough to see inside the cave. There had to be a landing. If she had to, if she could not swing clear over to it, she would grit her teeth and drop into the water, and if the shock didn't stop her heart, she'd swim for it. Once up on the dock, she'd search about for a boat.

Again and again she told herself that there had to be a boat, that Maartens would be sure to have one ready, in case he needed to get out of the house two steps ahead of the law. If Alma was right, if there actually were a cave . . . If she went all the way down only to find solid rock, what then?

She lay down on her bed to think. She could not climb down until she was absolutely clear in her mind as to what she would do when she reached the other end. She must decide now; once she was down at the bottom she would never in this world be able to climb back up. If she had to get into the water, she could undo her things and carry them under her left arm while she swam using her right. Not for any great distance, of course, but in one direction or the other along the cliff's face until she found a spot where she could come ashore.

On second thought, what good would her dress and cloak do her soaking wet? Only add to her discomfort. She wondered again how far Harwich was. Wet or dry, at least she'd have her shoes . . .

Getting up, she looked about the room. It was now or never. Why? "Now," she could drown as easily as get away. "Never?" That was overstating it, hadn't Maartens told her that very evening that the time would eventually come when she'd be free to go, when she could walk out the door under her own power?

And what made her think she could trust him? Then too, who could anticipate what complications might arise in the next few days? Nobody, least of all Charles and Gene Hampton, knew where she was, or if she was alive or dead. Of course Tom Burgess' body had been left at the site of the accident by Otto and certainly found by now. Mrs. Tyler knew Burgess had had a passenger and Charles would check with her . . . Perhaps trying to escape was all wrong. Charles and the police must be out looking for her. But then, they could have already come to Barringer House and been sent away by Maartens' lies.

No, it made no sense to wait any longer.

Reluctantly, she returned her reticule to the armoire, placing it alongside her mother's bag, and double-checking the knot around the bed leg, climbed up onto the windowsill. Gripping the rope firmly, she took a deep breath and started down. At once, the sea breeze slapped against her bare back, sending a tremor down her spine.

She could not look down. She would distract herself by counting the equidistant knots she had placed in the rope, stopping at every tenth one to rest, gripping the knot below with both insteps. Glancing upward, she could see the open window directly above. At any moment, she half expected Maartens to lean out, look down at her, grin and wave, produce a pair of shears and calmly snip the rope.

She closed her eyes to blot out the window, but the first picture her imagination produced was exactly what she expected, the water below and the white kite tail trailing down to it to her dress and cloak bundled at the end.

She had made her way down less than twenty feet when her upper arms began to grow weak, as if the blood were draining out of them replaced by water. Pausing to rest, she breathed deeply, shuddering against the cold. Lord, it was freezing! The wind whipped about her annoyingly, teasingly, like a bully circling her and touching her in the schoolyard. Far out to sea, a bellbuoy clanged and a ship's horn answered it.

Resuming her descent, she began to be buffeted by the wind, despite the weight below her. Again and again her knuckles and knees scraped against the granite wall of the cliff in front of her, but gritting her teeth and ignoring her discomfort she continued on down.

Time dragged by and her arms became weaker and weaker until at last she found herself barely ten feet above the bundle. The ocean had become louder as she drew closer to it and at this point a welcome change in the sound reached her ears.

Alma was right, there was a cave! As she moved down, her heart leaped at the sight of a wooden dock just inside the mouth of the cave, the water lapping against its barnacle-studded pilings, its near corner less than five feet from her!

She began swinging toward the cave and away from it, back and forth, back and forth . . . By now her arms ached furiously and her legs felt like ice. Swinging as wide as she could, she let go, landing in a heap on the corner of the dock one knee slipping over the edge nearly tumbling her into the dark water below. Pulling herself to her feet, she turned quickly to catch the bundle before the rope stopped swinging, but to her dismay it was just beyond her fingertips.

Let it hang, she thought, it could wait. First she'd locate a boat inside, get it started out and when she passed the bundle take it down.

She started down the dock and the further along she moved, the darker it became, the only sound the lapping of the water beneath her feet. Presently she was obliged to move over to the wall of the cave for fear of walking off. Feeling her way along the cave wall hand over hand she came at last to an opening. Crouching, she thrust one hand gingerly forward and found a series of stairs rising into the blackness. So far Alma's information was perfect. Pity she didn't know for a fact that Maartens had a boat tied up in readiness for a possible unscheduled departure.

What she wouldn't give for a match for a three-second look at her surroundings, but all she could do was continue to feel her way along the damp, rough wall and cross her fingers and hope that the boards beneath her feet would not suddenly end and her forward motion pitch her into the water. Pausing, she listened. There was a thumping sound only a few feet beyond, like a wooden mallet being struck against a cask, a slow but steady rhythm and with it the gentle slosh of water.

It was no mallet, the sound of the water confirmed it. It was a boat bumping against the dock. Hurrying forward, her eyes becoming accustomed to the darkness, she was able to distinguish the shape of the craft. It lay long and low in the water with two sets of oars across its two seats, what appeared to be a heavy wooden chest of some sort up near the bow and a single broken lobster pot on the floor near the stern.

If anything, she had even less experience with any sort of

boat than she had in distance swimming, being limited to a few Sunday afternoons on the Schuylkill River which wandered through the center of Philadelphia and which she much preferred to the equally placid but considerably wider Delaware on the east side of town. At that, she had never actually guided a boat on the Schuylkill, only rowing a bit for the sport of it while her escort of the afternoon or someone else steered. The waters outside the mouth of the cave posed a greater challenge than the Schuylkill River and were deeper, more powerful and filled with countless hazards that no river could boast.

How she wished Gene Hampton were with her now. He could handle a boat, she was sure, he was the sort of man who could handle anything, any emergency, any problem . . . even a Dr. Maartens.

But at that moment, Gene was miles away and she was on her own. And, now she thought about it, not doing badly so far. Wasn't the worst of it over, the descent into the maelstrom? Luckily the sea seemed to be continuing calm; had any waves been abroad she probably wouldn't even be able to get the boat out of the cave, let alone to land.

Getting into it with some difficulty, she managed to place two of the oars in the forward oarlocks, losing one extra one overboard in the process. Unfastening both stern and bowlines, she sat down and began rowing. The initial result was a great deal of splashing, slow turning one way then the other, and very little forward motion, until she got the hang of dipping both oar blades in at the same time and at just the right angle just deeply enough to gain the resistance needed to pull the bleat forward.

Splashing and roiling the water and bumping her way slowly along between the dock and the wall opposite, she neared the mouth of the cave and, hauling in both oars, stood up to turn around and locate her bundle hanging drawn from the bedroom window. Getting up from her seat too quickly, she nearly lost her balance and fell overboard, managing at the last instant to catch the gunwale and steady herself.

The boat drifted toward the bundle, clearly outlined in the moonlight by the entrance, but about ten feet from it it began veering off to the left away from the dock, drawn by the current. Picking up one of her oars, she began paddling canoe-fashion, so vigorously and so fast that she nearly turned the vessel around completely, heading the bow back the way she had come. After a great deal of struggling and hard labor better suited to a man with triple her strength, she managed to get the boat on course heading for the bundle. Grabbing it, she freed it, untying it hurriedly and getting into her dress, cloak and shoes. She wondered what was in the chest lying at the bottom of the boat, but her curiosity was no match for her desire to get to sea and up the coast as fast as she could. Settling down to rowing, she headed out of the cave as best she could, encountering continuing difficulty before finally turning to her left and making her way up the coast.

Although the sea was calm, waves rolled under the surface in a powerful undertow, threatening to seize the little boat, draw it back toward the cliff and shatter it into kindling. Changing her mind about heading up the coast, at least for the time being, she altered course and drove the vessel straight out to sea to a point nearly a hundred yards from shore. Her arms, weakened by the journey down the rope, tired easily and time after time she found it necessary to weigh her oars and rest.

The water surged beneath the boat in frightening fashion, as if an endless series of waves held in check by the patina of the surface threatened to burst through at any moment to swamp her completely.

The cliff rose moonward and in silhouette at its summit stood Barringer House, its chimneys like fingers probing the sky. She wondered if Otto was still up prowling about the house, if Devereaux had exchanged his snoring for a dream about Japanese screens, if Nurse Raphael was able to sleep at all. Now free of the place herself, she regretted her haste in destroying her note to Maartens. Telling him what she knew about him was small enough revenge for his holding her.

And yet even this distance out to sea, for some inexplicable reason she still could not feel entirely free of the house. From where it stood high on the rock, solitary and forbidding, filled to its eaves with a peculiar evil all its own, inhabited person for person by the strangest group of people she had ever met in her life, it seemed to reach out to her with invisible tendrils touching her and starting her skin crawling. No nightmare she could ever recall, no product of pickles and cheese or any other outrageous combination of foods could possibly match her experience wide awake in that awful house. In the future, whenever she got into her own bed at night with her door locked and hundreds of miles separating her from here, would she still be haunted by the memory of it?

She knew she would.

Barringer House, would that the cliff might open wide and swallow it!

Turning the bow of the boat so that the vessel moved on a line with the cliff, she rested fully a minute, then began pulling the oars with all the strength she could muster. Slowly, the house moved away from her, slipping back, gradually positioning itself over the left corner of the stern.

Water sloshed about the bottom of the boat, drenching her hems and her shoes. There was nothing to bail with, but fortunately no additional water seemed to be coming in, so ignoring it she concentrated on rowing, improving her ability, but gradually developing blisters on the palms and inside the fingers of both hands.

Weighing her oars, she rested again, trailing her smarting hands in the water to cool them. Then she began guiding the boat closer to land, noting that the cliff appeared to be diminishing in height, angling down toward level ground and beyond the shoreline what looked to be meadowland spotted here and there with tall weeds bending uniformly in the direction of the house.

The wind was stronger and colder out on the open water. It came at her back, biting through her cloak and dress, sending its chill fingers up her spine and across her shoulders. The water in the boat bottom continued to swirl and slosh about, finding its way into both her shoes and soaking her feet completely.

On and on she rower, until Barringer House was only a rough prominence breaking the line of the cliff top. Presently, hoping that she could find a safe place to put ashore, she made for land. The beach was strewn with rocks, the boat scraping bottom repeatedly as she neared it. Driving up onto the sand, she dropped her oars and, hurrying forward, got out of the boat, her heels swishing in the wet sand. Picking her way through the rocks, she made it up onto the grass and set out to look for the road.

It was now nearly three quarters of an hour since she had left the cave, and the world about continued deep in slumber. No lights were visible in any of the nearby houses, but even had there been there would be no purpose in stopping at any of them. Then, too, she had acquired a mistrust of strange houses. She must get to the hospital in Harwich as quickly as possible. Charles would probably not be on night duty, nor would Gene be there, but the hospital would be far easier to find than the house where Charles lived and first thing in the morning he'd surely come on duty. In the meantime, she'd be able to dry her feet, get a cup of tea, and hopefully an hour's sleep.

The wind grew bolder, the pliant maples creaking and swaying and the tall grasses in the meadow flattening to earth. Having walked a considerable distance during which time the moon vanished and reappeared several times, she arrived at a narrow road and starting down it, peered ahead looking for signs or a crossroad, some indication that she was headed for Harwich. There were no signs, however, save for a large, crudely lettered one mounted on a fence-post announcing that trespassers were unwelcome. Pausing to sit by the wayside to rest, she removed her wet shoes and massaged her feet. She could barely hear the ocean under the dominating sound of the night wind rising and falling and rising again, chasing aimlessly about. Once again the moon lost itself behind a lengthy column of clouds. But by this time her eyes had become used to the darkness and the road was easy to follow, although deeply rutted and filled with stones as it was, far from easy to travel. She had begun to develop blisters on the soles of both feet, painful and similar to those on her hands brought on by the rowing.

The road seemed to be edging back toward the shoreline and angling upward. Far ahead a large house showed itself. Her heart sank, even from a different point of view the outline was recognizable Barringer House! For the better part of an hour, instead of walking any from it she had been nearing it. Turning around, she started back the other way, trudging along without stopping, ignoring her aching feet and the wind swirling about wrapping her in its bitter cold.

No lights and no life appeared as on and on she walked. Reaching a crossroad, she made out two signs mounted on a post in the center, one pointing to Harwich. Following the name, however, was a single number that made her very nearly cry aloud in anguish.

8. Eight miles to Harwich. She rested under the sign, but the ground was uncomfortably cold and shortly she resumed her journey. She was making slower progress now, her feet having become badly swollen. Pausing, she removed her shoes and continued along in her wet stocking feet, along the shoulder of the road where the wild grasses were short, cut off or pounded down by coach and wagon traffic.

For two hours she walked, until the soles of her stockings wore away completely. But try as she was able, she could not get her shoes back onto her swollen feet. The sky was beginning to lose its blackness and she guessed that the sun would be up in an hour or less. No other signs appeared. Rural Maine was more than rural, she concluded, it was the frontier, untraveled, uninhabited, save for at most four houses including Barringer House since the beach.

She had no way of judging how far she had come, but assumed regretfully that if she hadn't gotten twisted about and wasted the time and energy it had taken her to walk back to within sight of the house she would be in Harwich now.

Force of will alone kept her going, but in spite of her resolve, in spite of her determined disregard for her physical discomfort, she at last reached a point where she could no longer go on. Slipping to the ground, she sat working her blistered feet with her hands, first one, then the other.

She had been sitting for nearly ten minutes when all at once she became aware of the faint sound of wheels turning and the slow, measured clomping of hooves. Looking back down the road through the graying darkness she spied an empty hay wagon coming, the driver perched high on his seat, his broad-brimmed hat flapping in the wind and a single jet black horse between the shafts tossing its head and snorting, clouds of vapor issuing from its nostrils like smoke from the windows of a burning building. Spying her, the driver cracked his whip over the horse, the wagon picked up speed and within seconds it was rattling up beside her.

"What have we here, Hagar in the wilderness, shoes in hand?" The man was heavy-set, his face puffed with age and reddened by the wind, but his eyes were friendly. "Who might you be, traipsing about at this hour?"

"My name is Alison Collier."

"Braden Gilyard is mine. What happened?"

"My gig lost a wheel and my horse ran away."

"Did he now!"

"I was on my way to Harwich."

Braden Gilyard had gotten down from his perch to help her up onto the seat, carrying on as he did so about the cold, the condition of her feet, and the need to get her to a doctor.

"Harwich? You're in luck. 'S'only a mile down the rud. Have you there in a jiffy."

"Would it be too much trouble to drop me at the hospital? I have a friend there."

"No trouble. Those feet of yours'll be needing 'tention. Hang on tight to the seatside, here we go!"

The wagon took off down the road, creaking and joggling, the horse seemingly grateful for the chance to stretch its legs and show off. They reached Harwich in short order. The town, assembled around the single main street dividing it, was mainly gray and newly-painted white wooden buildings snuggled together like quail in a thicket. A few industrious housewives were up, and holystoning their stoops, and a gentleman early riser in an expensive suit and beaver stood at the blacksmith's door pounding loudly and calling out, but most of the homes were still curtained and dark against the lingering night shadows. A coach passed by rocking over the narrow road, bouncing its sleeping passengers against one another like tumbling ninepins.

The hospital was situated at the far end of town, a large white frame building two stories high, its double front door tightly closed, its windows unlit, but a side door standing ajar as if to welcome her.

A nurse came to the door in answer to Braden Gilyard's summons, a young woman sleepy-eyed and starchily attired, her cap clinging to her hair with no visible assistance. She called a second nurse and the two of them helped Alison inside, she murmuring her thanks to Gilyard and all but collapsing from exhaustion.

5

"I didn't have the heart to wake you."

She had opened her eyes and the sound of Charles' voice opened them again. Her mouth was dry and felt swollen, cheeks, gums, even her tongue; she ached all over, as if a great invisible weight were pressing her down, but his voice and his smiling presence hovering over her filled her with comfort and relief.

"What time is it?"

"Nearly five. Getting dark outside. Do you feel up to talking?"

"There's so much to tell you'll be here all night."

"First, are you hungry?"

"Not really, just terribly thirsty." He poured water for her and she propped herself up on both elbows to drink. The bed in which she lay was metal and narrow and the bedclothes smelled of disinfectant, but the bed itself was cozy and comfortable. Two gas lamps burning against the far wall threw gray shadows across the ceiling and through the two windows to her right she could see the twilight gathering about a stand of oaks.

Hers was the only bed in the room. Charles took her hand, patting it gently.

"I telegraphed your mother telling her you're safe and well and you'll be home in two or three days."

"Poor mother, she must be beside herself."

"So, here you are. Mind telling me how you got here?"

"I started out from the Speedwell the night of the storm. There was an accident, the driver was killed . . ."

"Slowly, slowly. Gene and I and the search party found the wreckage of the coach and Tom Burgess' body, but where did you disappear to?"

"Two men from Barringer House rescued me."

"Barringer House. I thought so. Would you believe it, that was the very first place we went to. They claimed they hadn't seen you and of course we had no assurance you were there, so we couldn't demand to search the house."

She began to unravel the strange sequence of events culminating in Dr. Maartens' decision to hold her.

"He kidnapped me! He ought to be arrested, all of them should! I mean you can't just hold somebody against his will!"

Charles pondered a moment. "I don't know, Alison, I'm no lawyer and I could be wrong, but it might be difficult to prove that he actually held you there."

"He did, I tell you!"

"But, don't you see, it would be his word against yours. And he's a doctor, he could easily claim that you weren't yet fit to travel, that after examining you he simply decided to keep you there an extra day or two."

"I suppose. But there's more, lots more."

She went into a detailed description of the ceremony. As she continued, Charles' eyes widened in amazement, but there was an undisguisable twinkle in them.

"Fantastic!"

"You don't believe a word!"

He shrugged and smiled and, getting up from where he had been sitting alongside her bed, went to the window and looked out.

"You said yourself you'd gotten quite a blow on the head . . ."

"I didn't dream it, Charles. I tell you I saw the start of the thing one night, before that monster attacked me, and the entire business the next night, start to finish. A dead girl brought back to life! It took three hours."

"All right, if you say so, but only because I'm enormously broad-minded and because you're so depressingly serious about the thing. Just let's keep things in perspective."

"I am!"

"This fellow you say is responsible, this Dr. Maartens, you seem to think he's broken the law. From all I can see, if he and the others did what you claim they did, there's nothing much illegal about it. If the man and woman watching were the girl's parents, obviously they gave their consent . . ."

"But you can't dig bodies up from graves and just bring them back to life. It isn't Christian!"

Charles laughed at her indignation and her choice of words and she herself could scarcely suppress a smile when she thought about what she'd said.

"I don't know," he murmured, "it all sounds so utterly fantastic."

"Is that all you can say?"

"What do you want me to say? What other word is there to describe it, except perhaps incredible . . ."

"Unbelievable is what you mean. All right, it's not illegal or if it is the good outweighs the bad, but what about the newspaper clipping in that Arctic book?"

"Ah, cousin dear, there you have something. You're sure the description tallies with Maartens?"

"Absolutely! Besides, why else would Devereaux hang onto it?"

"It's definitely something the police should know about."

"Can't Maartens be arrested?"

"He can certainly be held for questioning. I'm sure the Albany police would be interested in talking to him. Fantastic . . ."

"You still think I am lying, don't you, making it all up out of whole cloth."

"No, really, I'm just stunned by it all." Again he sat down beside her. "You've certainly been through the mill, haven't you?"

"I wouldn't want to go through it again, I'll tell you that. Is Gene here?"

"Hampton? No, he's been away since the day after the storm. Won't be back till Friday."

"I've lost all track of time. What's today?"

"Tuesday, the eleventh."

"In a way, it all seems like it happened in one night. You don't think my mind is affected, do you?" she asked, laughing.

"No, but if I were you I wouldn't bruit this about. Other people around here might not be so tolerant. How far did you walk?"

"Look at my feet, and you tell me."

He lifted the bedclothes and examined the soles of her feet. "Lovely, did you come from Massachusetts or Canada?"

"How many blisters?"

"Seven, including a couple as big as your eyes. But nothing two or three days off your feet won't cure. When I leave, I'll send a nurse in to bathe them with brine, prick those that aren't broken already and dry them out. We'll have you shipshape in no time. That bastard!"

"Charles!"

"I mean it. I don't know what the law can do to him and I don't particularly care, but he's not getting off without answering to this! I've a good mind to forget about the local police, bypass them and contact the Albany police directly. It's terrible, you come up here for your poor father's funeral, you run into one devil of a storm and get waylaid in that damned mausoleum and end up in a hospital bed! And all my fault!"

"Don't be ridiculous, it's my own fault. If I'd listened to Mrs. Tyler and stayed at the Speedwell overnight . . ."

"The whole thing was so damned unnecessary." He calmed down and studied her. "Tell me again about this business with the dead girl. She was dead . . . not just bluffing."

"She was dead. You can tell, I mean I saw daddy only a few hours earlier and they looked as alike as two peas in a pod, the face, the flesh . . . no breathing, none."

"These other people, the other doctor and the nurse."

"They were as strange as he was. Devereaux lost his license to practice for . . . you know."

"Malpractice?"

"That's it and the nurse, Raphael, Rayfield, whatever her name is . . . come to think of it she may not even be a real nurse at all, not that that makes any difference. The whole thing was like some outlandish masquerade ball, everybody wearing a false face."

"Thank goodness you got out of there in one piece. I'll pick it up from here on. And unless you can come up with a better idea I'm getting in touch with the Albany police."

Taking a thermometer out of a small case, he shook it twice and inserted it in her mouth.

"What's this for?"

"Sssh . . ."

He took her pulse as he waited. She was impressed, he was suddenly so businesslike, so professional and so reassuring. She counted herself very lucky that despite her ordeal everything had come out all right. And all she'd come away with would be a few unpleasant memories, two tender feet and promise of a cold. As if to remind her of the latter probability, no sooner was the thermometer removed than she sneezed loudly.

"You're running a slight fever." He listened to her chest with his stethoscope. "And you've got what you might expect to get wandering the countryside in your bare feet in October . . ."

"Pneumonia?"

"No such luck. At least it doesn't appear to be. You're a much too hardy specimen. You'll have to settle for the plain old sniffles. You stay tucked in bed, we'll fill you full of soup, make you sleep fifteen hours a day, and lavish you with attention and you'll be good as new before you know it."

"I'm grateful, Charles, if it weren't for you . . ."

"Don't talk nonsense. It's purely selfish on my part. I'd like to get this whole business off my conscience."

"I tell you you're not to blame!"

"If Gene and I hadn't left the inn, if we'd stayed with you until it was time for your train it never would have happened."

"If, if . . ."

Bending, he kissed her on the forehead. "We'll talk about it later."

"Oh, Lord!"

"What's the matter?"

"You sound just like Maartens."

"I'd like to make his acquaintance, in a room about the size of this one, with the door locked and just the two of us." His eyes narrowed, he thought a moment and then smiled. "Relax, doze, dream sweet dreams, I must see to a patient. It's after five, I'll be back in an hour or so. We'll have a bite of supper together. In the meanwhile, I'll get a nurse in here to tend to your lovely feet. And give you something for your cold."

Again he kissed her on the forehead and, pausing in the doorway to wave, went out the door. Minutes later a nurse came in, gave her two pink pills to swallow and then set about tending to her feet and bathing them in a tepid solution of salt water. The newcomer was short, pinch-waisted and pretty. And thoroughly Scottish, from her red hair and freckles to her blue eyes and burr.

"You must have walked a hoondred miles. It's nothing serious, though. My name's Mary Elizabeth MacIntosh, what's yours?"

"Alison Collier."

"Collier. Are you related to the doctor?"

"Cousins."

"Lucky you. Handsome devil, ain't he? Every nurse in the hospital's got an eye out for him, even the old crows. He's sweet, too, a real gentleman. Not like some of them around here, not mentioning any names. Some doctors can be bad as patients when it comes to hanky panky and annoyance. Not that I don't know how to handle myself. Some of the girls have their hands full and daren't turn their backs, but not yours truly. You've a cold coming, haven't you, dear? Bed rest is best for that, better than any pink pills, I can tell you. Thing about a cold is, you don't want it to get out of hand. Keep it light and away it goes in two shakes of a lamb's tail. Let it settle in your chest and you'll cough and carry on for a month of Sundays. Did you hear the news?"

"What?"

"About the boat and the money."

"I haven't heard a thing."

"It happened this morning. A sma' boat with the oars still in it was found beached. A wee lad found it, no name on it, no markings of any sort, just a bashed-in lobster pot and a box. Being a lad, being human he was curious and he opened the box and guess what he found? Nearly twenty thousand dollars! Can you imagine?"

"Where did you say this boat was found?"

"On the shore, up the way from Barringer House."

Twenty thousand dollars! Just as she had guessed, Maartens had kept the boat in the cave in case he needed to get away in a hurry, out to a waiting sloop or some other, larger vessel that could take the lot of them out of the country, if need be! And he'd hidden his money in the box, money no doubt given him by the blond girl's parents for "services rendered," they and who knew how many others!

Talk about revenge . . . without even suspecting it, she had slipped away with every penny, leaving it in the boat for the "wee lad" to find. Maartens would be absolutely furious, he must be already! How lovely!

"Twenty thousand?"

"Aye, and no exaggeration. I got it from the head nurse who is intimate friends with the wife of the neighbor of the man whose stepson it was found it."

"And what will they do with the money?"

"I was wondering that myself. We were discussing it, the head nurse and I and a couple of the others. Finders keepers everybody seems to think, unless the rightful owner comes forward. But who can claim such an enormous amount is his? What proof can he offer? There was no name on the boat, no markings of any sort. Looked like every other boat like it and there's hoondreds up and down the coast, thousands!"

"Nothing in the box to indicate who owned it?"

"Ha, if there was now the wee lad was bright enough to get rid of it. Fascinating story, though, ain't it?"

"A beautiful story."

"I know what I'd do if I ever got these hands on a fortune that size, I'd spend every copper. I'd buy frocks and capes and coats and shoes and a Sunday gig and two spanking bay horses tall as eavestroughs. I'd have me a time, I would. And no man'd diddle me out of any of it with sweet talk and smiles and suchlike . . ."

Maartens would be furious, livid! How she wished she might see his face when he heard the news. And how Devereaux, if he were the one to find out, would enjoy announcing it, in spite of his own loss, for it had to belong to all of them.

Nurse Mary Elizabeth MacIntosh was full of information, about finding the money, about the hospital, about Charles.

"A lovely man. One I wouldn't mind sharing my fortune with. So upright and respectable, and a marvelous doctor. Very sure of himself in surgery. Not cocky like some, but confident. He took a gall bladder out just last week, neat as a pin. Easy as taking your foot out of your shoe. I helped assist. Oh, what a difference that ether makes. Ten years ago there was no such thing. Head nurse says they used to put patients out with everything under the sun, even a mallet I shouldn't wonder. But your Dr. Collier is very good. And so good looking, la-de-da!"

The nurse went away and Alison lay in bed turning over the events of the past few days. Perhaps Charles was right in wanting to contact the Albany police. Let them handle Maartens.

Dear Charles, so upset over what had happened to her,

so quick to take the blame when it was wholly undeserved. She imagined what it would have been like to have to come to Maine for the funeral without him there to prepare everything, to assist her every step of the way and to take care of her now when she needed him most.

He brought supper in for the two of them, turkey, mashed potatoes drowned in gravy and green beans, with a somewhat unappetizing-looking pudding for dessert.

"Looks like mud, doesn't it?" he said ruefully. "Our table isn't quite up to Barringer House, I'm afraid, but the company's an improvement."

They ate and joked together until she turned the conversation down a serious avenue.

"You said that Gene is away?"

"In Boston, on business for the hospital. Be back on Friday."

"Too bad, I expect I'll be home by then."

"You will be."

"I would have liked to have seen him."

"Rather like the old reprobate, don't you?"

"He's not old and I'm sure he's no reprobate."

"Little do you know, child."

"A nice thing to say about your best friend."

"I must warn you before you get involved, Alison. He's been married seven times and has ten, no eleven children—I forgot baby Cynthia. And he can be absolutely vicious when he's drunk. A raving maniac. But that's only every night, during the day he's a prince of a fellow."

"You're nasty. You're just jealous of him, I can tell."

"Can you now? Seriously, though, you do like him."

"As a friend, of course."

"Oh, come now, every time a girl says 'as a friend' she means a lot more than a friend. Isn't that so? Of course. Remember, my dear, you're talking to a doctor, a brilliant mind, if I do say so myself. I can read your mind like a book."

"All right, what am I thinking about right now, this very moment?"

"Let me see . . . you're thinking about seeing Gene, bumping into him accidentally. He'll take you to lunch . . ."

"Did the nurse say anything about my feet?" she asked, reddening slightly.

"Good Lord, can't that wait till we finish eating?" He made a face and cackled laughter. "Maybe I shouldn't say it, but Gene rather likes you."

"What did he say about me?"

"The usual, beautiful, intelligent . . . or was it brilliant? Delight to be with . . ."

"Oh, stop it!"

They finished eating and he visited with her until after seven when an orderly appeared asking to speak with him. They talked in undertones in the doorway and Charles excused himself.

At eight-thirty Mary Elizabeth MacIntosh reappeared, with a glass filled with suspicious-looking clear liquid.

"Laudanum, tincture of opium, you're to drink every drop. You'll sleep like a bairn."

"I really don't need it."

"Doctor's orders. Let me bathe your feet again."

She did so and went away, carrying her basin filled with a salt solution with the dignity and aplomb of a deacon walking his collection plate up the aisle to the altar. At nine she came in to turn down the lamps and fluff her pillow, and after she'd gone, Alison raised herself on her right elbow and reached across with her left hand to the night table for the laudanum. The position was awkward and in picking it up, she slipped, spilling most of it on the floor before managing to right the glass. Annoyed, she downed what was left, put the glass back on the table, lay back and closed her eyes.

Visions of Gene Hampton came to her, his flaming hair, his smile . . . So he thought her beautiful. She'd never thought herself beautiful, pretty, perhaps, but not beautiful. And yet who was she to argue? At that it was probably just more nonsense talk from Charles, to make her feel good. Eleven children indeed!

It would be so good to get home and see mother up and about again. And what a story she had to tell everyone, although why anyone would believe a word of it was beyond her. Her mother would believe her, and Lydia, the maid, and the whole world actually, if Charles followed through as he intended and contacted the Albany police. Unless, of course, Maartens got away.

She yawned as the narcotic began to dull her senses. More than relieved by the final outcome, she was, she told herself, blissfully happy. Just to be able to fall asleep knowing that her worries were ended, that at long last, all was right with her world.

6

When she opened her eyes, she was at once conscious of the familiarity of her surroundings, although at first she could see nothing except the open door just beyond the foot of her bed. Her awareness was a feeling rather than recognition. Then, like a needle of ice piercing her heart, she realized the truth.

She was back in Barringer House! But, as her mind—wrapped in the wool of semi-consciousness—accepted this, she could not even gasp reaction. Closing her eyes, praying that it was a dream, a nightmare that would vanish in seconds, she opened them again.

It was no nightmare. It was her room, her prison cell, the table in the corner, the mirror above it, the armoire against the wall to her right, and standing at the window looking out into the moonless night, cousin Charles. He started to turn around as footsteps sounded in the corridor and immediately she closed her eyes, pretending to sleep.

"What the devil . . ." Maartens' voice, how well she knew it. "What are you doing here?"

"What does it look like, Hendrik? I've brought back your wandering house guest."

"Great God!"

"Relax, doctor. Look at you, you're shaking. You're pale as a ghost!"

"Why bring her back here?"

"What do you suggest I do with her, hold her in the hospital so she can blab her story to everyone who'll listen, put her on her train to Philadelphia? No, thank you. She's your responsibility, my friend!"

"What are we getting excited about?"

"You're getting excited, I'm not."

"She doesn't know anything . . ."

"She knows everything. She saw the whole business with the Gately girl, from beginning to end!"

"That's impossible!"

"She described it to me down to the last fine detail. She watched every move for three solid hours from the doorway of a room over the railing."

"I don't believe it!"

"You'd better. You've messed things up marvelously this time!"

"Let's go downstairs, we can't talk here, she may wake up."

"She won't wake up. She's had enough laudanum to keep her under till tomorrow noon. How do you think I was able to get her out of the hospital in the dead of night, into a carriage and back here without her waking? You are a stupid man. You know that, don't you!"

"She took our boat, all our money . . ."

"Your money, not mine." The edge to Charles' voice was as unnerving as his words. It was a different voice, a different person, one far removed from the Charles she knew and liked so much. A hard and cynical man enjoying his chance to bully Maartens, thoroughly out of patience with the older man's blundering. And a coward, fearful that Maartens' mistakes and oversights would form a rope that would pull the two of them down into the mire.

"We've got to talk," said Maartens nervously.

"We are talking!" thundered Charles, "although you

seem to have little to say that makes any sense. What are you going to do with her?"

"I planned on letting her go, just before we left . . . but now she knows too much. We'll have to get rid of her."

"No you don't! Not a chance, you'll not harm her!"

Maartens' voice rose, taking on a tone of confidence. And just as quickly Charles retreated to the defensive.

"We either get rid of her or we let her go," said the older man. "It's a very simple choice. If she dies our little secret is safe. If she lives we go to prison for life, if they don't hang us. You choose to give up your life to save hers, you have my blessing. But John and Constance and I aren't in your shoes. She means nothing to us."

"Good God, if only we didn't have to!"

"But we do."

"All thanks to your bungling. Why in hell did you have to pull her out of that damned coach in the first place?"

"Ask John, he and Otto did it. They dropped her in my lap."

"If this doesn't beat the devil! We had a perfect plan working for us. Three times without a hitch. Suddenly she shows up and all hell breaks loose. Damn it all!"

"If getting rid of her bothers you that much . . ."

"All right, all right, all right, do what you have to. Don't tell me, I don't want to know about it."

"You're getting all upset over nothing. Mistakes have been made, I'm not denying that. She's a clever girl, not the faint-hearted type, putty-in-your-hands damsel in distress. She tricked us handily. The problem exists, admittedly, but it's easily solved and I shall solve it."

"Don't let that ogre Otto get his hands on her!"

"Trust me, I'll take care of everything my own way. My pleasure. I'm out a great deal of money thanks to her. I like money very much, almost as much as you do. Losing all that lovely cash is hard to take."

"It's all very upsetting . . ."

"Is it really, is this a physician I hear?"

"Don't start anything, Hendrik, I'm not in the mood."

"Only teasing, doctor. But seriously, now you're here, let's talk business. Do you have anything for us?"

"Not now. Besides, I'm in no mood for work, not when a damned infernal machine explodes smack in my face!"

"Pity, I'd like very much to recoup my losses as quickly as possible."

"I'm going . . ."

"Not right away. I want you to look at Vera."

"The old woman?"

"She's very ill. I'm afraid we're going to lose her."

"What's the trouble?"

"A bronchial condition. We've put her to bed, but she's losing strength and neither John nor I seem to be able to do anything for her."

"I'm not surprised. Answer me one question, Hendrik, something I've always been tempted to ask you. What earthly use is your friend Devereaux?"

"Don't underestimate him, Charles. At one time he was an excellent doctor."

"At one time. Right now he's an excellent drunk. Your loyalty to him is touching, but why you bother I'll never know."

"You seem to forget it's no simple matter selecting members for our little circle. We're not exactly a Masonic lodge, you know."

"I know."

"My, we are upset, aren't we? Your attitude is all wrong, my friend. For the sort of money you're earning you really ought to expect to put up with a bit of inconvenience now and then."

"Is that what you call it? You're a damned fool, Hendrik!"

"You have already so informed me. Will you look at Vera?"

"I suppose. Exactly how old is she?"

"At least eighty."

"Three score and ten, doctor. Who are we to postpone the inevitable? Can't she be replaced?"

"I've already spoken to Constance, but she adamantly refuses to even consider it. Besides, she wouldn't be right for the part. At that, even if she agreed, we'd have to replace her in turn. John and I can't work without a nurse."

"Where did you find the old woman?"

"In Rotterdam."

"Maybe you'd better go back there and get her sister."

"Look at her, that's all I ask."

"What about bringing her to the hospital?"

"She's too weak."

"My, you do have your problems, don't you, doctor?"

"Yes indeed, but my problems are your problems, my friend."

The two of them went out of the room. As soon as the door closed and locked behind them, Alison got out of bed and, teetering slightly, made her way to the window. There'd be no going down a rope this time. The drape pulls were gone and the bedsheets ripped in two and tied together wouldn't hang halfway down. There was a quick way down, but she could easily kill herself attempting it. At that, it might be preferable to what Maartens had in store for her.

Dear Charles, so upset over what had happened to her, so quick to take the blame when it was wholly undeserved.

What a blind fool she had been, what a naive and unsuspecting innocent! But how could he sink so low? To ally himself with a man like Maartens, for money . . . risking prison or even the hangman's noose? Her staunchest protector, her only protector in this alien place, one of them!

What the lot of them were up to, the dead girl, the ceremony, the money, all of it suddenly paled into insignificance. Overshadowing it all was the immediate threat to her life. They meant to kill her, they had to protect themselves.

The inevitability of death was something she had never really thought about. Young people rarely bothered to; they were too busy living to dwell on dying. But dying, lying in bed and watching the black angel creeping up on you, like darkness creeping across the land, is one thing. To be murdered in cold blood, to know it's entered in the book, that nothing can forestall it and not to know when or how, had to be infinitely worse.

And worse it was, for her. There it was in front of her, the blackest picture the eye can see, but with a pinpoint of light revealing itself.

Time. She had until noon the next day to do what she could to save herself. Charles, Aunt Kate's devoted son, handsome, good-hearted Charles, had taken it for granted she'd drunk all the laudanum the nurse had given her, telling Maartens confidently that she'd sleep till noon. So she had more than eleven hours to plan and effect her second escape from Barringer House.

Opening the window, she let it swing and leaning out, looked straight down. She could hear the ocean better than she could see it; the water was rough, waves pounding in rapid succession against the base of the cliff, in sharp contrast to the calm of the previous night. Swimming would be extremely difficult, but it looked to be her only chance. If she fashioned a rope out of the sheets and the blanket got halfway down and dropped the rest of the way . . .

Why dwell on it, do it! But no sooner had she decided than a key turned in the door and it opened, revealing Nurse Raphael.

"Welcome back, my dear. Up and about I see. You gave us quite an exciting day."

"What do you want, Mrs. Rayfield?"

"You're moving. Dr. Maartens doesn't think this room suits you." She stepped aside and Otto came lumbering in. Alison backed against the wall and began screaming, but it was useless. Picking her up as easily as he might have picked the pillow up off the bed, he carried her out the door and down the corridor, the nurse trailing behind them, candle high.

Through the corridor door they went, down the way full length, down the stairs to the foyer and reversing direction back through the house. Down more stairs to the cellar and a storeroom, Otto dropping her unceremoniously. Then he backed away giggling, permitting Nurse Raphael to come in. Bending, she let wax drip on the stone floor, set the candle in it and went out, locking the padlock on the door.

She looked about. The room appeared half the size of her bedroom. Against the wall opposite the door, shelves were stacked three high, with a bushel basket partially filled with apples on each shelf. A blanket had been flung on the lower shelf. Getting to her feet, she pushed the basket of apples to one end and climbed onto the shelf, pulling the blanket over her. She would lie down to conserve her strength, but she would not sleep. She would instead let the candle burn itself out while she put her intelligence to work conceiving a way to escape.

But the longer she thought about it, the stronger the persuasion became that escape from this room was out of the question. The only possible exit was the door and the lock on it could hardly be picked through solid wood, even if she'd had something to pick with.

She could start the door on fire! Burn away enough of it to make a hole to crawl through. Jumping up, she jerked the blanket to wrap it around her, but in doing so upset the half-filled basket of apples at her feet, overturning it, apples tumbling out, scattering across the floor upending the candle and extinguishing the flame.

Lying down again she turned on her right side, snuggling the blanket around her. What now? Excepting dear Charles, nobody on the outside had the faintest idea where she was. Nurse MacIntosh would show up for duty in the morning and find her bed empty or somebody else in it and would probably be told by Charles that his cousin was on her way home.

Gene Hampton . . . he knew nothing beyond the fact that the coach had overturned and she had disappeared. By the time he got back from Boston it would be all over.

If Alma brought her breakfast maybe she could overpower her. But if Otto showed up . . . Damn! What had she done in her lifetime to deserve this? She'd never harmed a soul, least of all Charles or Maartens or any of them. She hadn't even been conscious when Devereaux and Otto had brought her to Barringer House. And as for the business with the Gately girl, she wasn't the least bit interested, not really, curious maybe, who wouldn't be curious?

What difference did it make, anyway? Nobody seemed to give two pins about what was fair and what wasn't, her rights and her welfare. She was going to die, just as surely as the sun rose. That it wasn't fair, that it shouldn't be, was meaningless, she was as good as dead and buried already.

And with Charles' blessing.

She tried to screw up her courage, but with little success; she began to hear her heart beating, the palms of her hands became clammy cold and her mouth turned dry. How, she wondered, would Charles go about justifying her sudden disappearance from the hospital? As far as that went who knew she was even there, except MacIntosh, the orderly and the two nurses who'd met her at the door? And Braden Gilyard, her Good Samaritan. The hospital help would accept whatever explanation Charles gave them, without questioning it. And why shouldn't they? Certainly none of them would dream of suspecting him of any wrongdoing, not handsome, gifted, outrageously respectable Charles Collier. As for Mr. Gilyard, he'd gone on his way assuming she'd be properly cared for. By now her name and her face were already fading from his memory.

Dawn arrived, slender shafts of gray light slipping in through an unseen cellar window filtering through narrow cracks in the stout wooden door.

In spite of herself she dozed off just as the day began and was wakened by the loud scraping of the door opening. Nurse Raphael entered smiling icily, Otto wavering behind her. She carried a cup of tea, holding its saucer like a precious offering being raised to some deity.

"Get the apples out of here," she said to Otto and he carried the baskets out the door, kicking out the apples scattered across the floor and pocketing what remained of the candle.

"Is this my sumptuous breakfast?" asked Alison.

"All we can spare, my dear. Pity you were so shortsighted."

"I didn't plan on coming back, if that's what you mean."

"I mean you should have stuffed yourself with apples

while you could. Too late now."

"So that's it, I'm to be starved to death."

The woman laughed, throwing her head back, the tea sloshing over the lip of the cup onto the saucer as she jerked her hands. It was hot and some of it ran down her fingers, burning her. Cursing, she threw cup and saucer to the floor, smashing them.

"Take a good look, this will be the last you'll see of any of us!"

"I want something to eat! I demand it!"

"You want, you demand . . . Let me tell you something, Miss Collier, the mood the doctor's in this very moment losing all that money, you're lucky he doesn't come down here with his pistol!"

They left. The day lengthened, morning interminably long and boring dragging its way to noon hour and into the afternoon, the hands on her watch crawling around the face.

She had no more visitors that day, not even Alma, the nosiest, the most curious of all. That night she slept fitfully, her stomach growling for nourishment, alternately angry and softly pleading. But no food was brought to her and nothing to drink, not that night nor all the next day.

By Friday morning her hunger had become ravenous. Maartens' failure to appear, to check on her and satisfy himself that she was beginning to suffer in earnest surprised her. But then, perhaps Nurse Raphael was right, perhaps she should be grateful that he stayed away, if he was that upset over the loss of his twenty thousand dollars.

Early in the afternoon she heard footsteps coming down the cellar stairs and she called out, but whoever it was paid no attention to her and after traipsing about ostensibly looking for something, found it or didn't and went back upstairs.

She sat on the floor and weighed her predicament. In all the days of her life she had never gone a single one without food; here and now she was midway through her third day without so much as a taste of the tea spilled early Wednesday morning. Wednesday, Thursday, Friday . . . Gene Hampton would be returning from Boston today, for all the good it would do her. She wondered if he'd thought about her disappearance; he must be worried about her, and yet as far as that went she'd thought Charles had been concerned, beside himself actually. She'd believed his every word, including his announcement that he'd telegraphed her mother.

Looking on the black side of it, what made her think Gene wasn't as deeply involved as Charles? Certainly no two men were closer. The mere suggestion that Gene was as knowledgeable of the situation, as deeply implicated and as guilty as Charles gave her a queasy feeling.

Oh, what a lovely planet her world was!

Someone was coming down the stairs. Again she called out, but there was no answer. Then the padlock was opened and the door. Dr. Devereaux.

"Miss Alison Collier of Philadelphia, I believe."

He was sober, unkempt looking as usual, in need of a shave, his eyes glazed with exhaustion, but he had not been drinking.

"Please, please, get me something to eat!"

Sympathy flooded his face and coming into the little room he took her by the arms and eased her against the wall.

"Here, here . . ."

"They're starving me . . ."

"Who?"

"Maartens."

"Lie down, I'll go up to the kitchen and get you something."

"Hurry, please!"

"Patience, I'll be down as quickly as I can. I'm going to have to lock you up, though, in case any of them comes snooping around. Of all the bloody idiocy!"

He went away muttering, mercifully returning within minutes with a loaf of black bread and half a cold chicken wrapped in a napkin. Seizing the chicken she attacked it.

"Slowly, slowly, you'll make yourself sick and chuck it all up. And careful of the bones. You say our mutual friend did this to you?"

She began relating what had happened, but almost immediately he stopped her.

"I know all that. I know also that Louis isn't starving you."

"Nurse Raphael . . ."

He nodded. "That sounds more like it. I wouldn't put it past the dear girl."

"She despises me, I can tell by the way she stares at me."

"She despises the entire human race, herself in particular."

Alison talked while she ate, tearing pieces out of the bread and cramming them into her mouth voraciously, fleetingly reminding herself of the exhibition put on by Otto at the kitchen table on her first "visit" to Barringer House.

"She adores you. The harder you are on her, the more she loves you."

"I can't stand the woman. She's always touching me, that icy claw of hers on my wrist, patting my bloody cheek. Damned masochist, that's what she is." He paused. "Say, did you get a chance to look around down here before they locked you up?"

"Not really."

"Damn! We're fresh out of rum. Reason I came down here, hoping there might be a half-filled cask or two lying about, neglected by the years. I'm so thirsty my tongue's cracking."

"I haven't seen any rum. What is he going to do with me?"

Devereaux's face clouded and he shook his head. "Nothing you're going to appreciate, I'm afraid. Rules of the game. We're finished here, the old woman's dead, the lid's about to pop off, your cousin and Louis have been at each other's throats two nights running now. Louis is furious over your running off with his money. I'd wager we'll be moving on soon."

"But how can he go without any money?"

Devereaux laughed. "That's funny. My dear Alison Collier, the man is rich as Croesus. He's got bank accounts scattered all over the bloody northeast. And the shattering irony of it is I'm the one who put him up on his golden pedestal." He tapped his forehead with his index finger. "My idea, the whole scheme, beginning to end and most of the refinements to boot."

"Bringing people back from the dead?"

"Exactly."

"He intends to leave me here locked up, doesn't he?"

"Something like that."

"Will you help me?"

He shook his head, grinning self-consciously. "I help you, you'll help put a bloody rope round my neck."

"You're wrong. Think about it."

"I am, I can't help you, little miss. Stealing food for you is as far as I can go. That's simple Christian charity, but committing suicide for you is a little beyond my capabilities. Sorry, really am."

"Sooner or later he's going to get caught, you all are. You know that, it's at the back of your mind constantly, you can't deny it. But if you give evidence against him, you can get off. They'll let you off in a minute. It always works that way."

"No, thank you. It's hard enough for me to look in my shaving mirror now without playing Judas Iscariot."

"You think he's Jesus? You think he deserves your loyalty?"

"Eat."

"You hate him, you know you do."

"Let's say we're not as close as we used to be."

"You can't stand him. Why else keep that clipping from the Albany newspaper?"

"Ah-hah, so it was you who took it!"

"No. I saw it, I read it, the night I eavesdropped on your little theatrical performance. I was leafing through your Arctic book and it dropped to the floor."

"And you didn't take it?"

"I did not. I put it right back where I found it."

"Funny, just an hour ago I was looking for it. Got to thinking it was a bloody stupid place to hide it. Damned incriminating."

"Of course. You kept it, you wanted something you could hold over his head, didn't you!"

"You never know when something like that might come in handy. No honor among thieves and all that. But look here, if it wasn't you who took it it was either him or Constance."

"Not her. She'd have no need of it, she wouldn't do anything to hurt you, not the way she feels about you."

"Maybe she'd want it for her own protection. She doesn't exactly idolize the bastard, you know."

"Will you help me escape? All you have to do is leave the door unlocked."

He thought a moment, then slowly shook his head. “I can’t. We’re in so deep now, we’ve carried this thing so bloody far that if the bottom drops out, if I let you loose and you help kick it out we’ll be done for. Oh, maybe I’ll beat the rope if I testify, but they’ll never let me off, never.”

“They will, they’ll have to, I’ll tell them everything. I can make you look like a hero!”

“No. I’ve got to go now.”

He went to the door, turned and stared at her pityingly. “I’m sorry, you must believe that. Wish me luck, I’ve got to find me some strong drink! Got to!”

Chortling, he closed the door, locking it.

7

Early in the evening he came back, waving a bottle of rum triumphantly.

"Look what I found! Bloody gift of the gods sitting on my bureau! She loves me, she loves me . . ."

"You'll help me, you've got to . . ."

"Can't. Not possible. Just came down for a little decent conversation. What do you think of this?"

Pulling the cork and flinging it to the floor, he traced the label with his finger, mumbling.

"Doctor . . ."

"Ssssh. Don Alfredo. Never heard of it. Who cares, a thirsty man never quibbles over labels." Taking a swig, he lowered the bottle. "Bitter, rotten grapes, but oh so warming going down. It's not the during, anyway, it's the after. Every respectable sot knows that!"

"Listen to me, if you leave the door open and I get out no one will ever know it was you did it."

"I'd know. Anyway, what's the difference whether they knew or not, we'd all wind up behind bars, me in the dampest cell."

"He's going to leave me here to die. Do you approve? Is that what you want? Me on your conscience the rest of your life?"

"Please, if that's all you can talk about there's no point in my staying. Be a good girl, change the bloody subject."

It was useless. He may have been basically decent, for all his complexes, for all his pretense, but he was either mortally afraid of crossing Maartens, or just as afraid of being caught and hanged. He took two more swigs frown the bottle in quick succession, grinning like a devil, blissfully oblivious of her distress. Then abruptly, in a single second his smile vanished, replaced by utter dread.

"Rum, rum . . ."

"What's the matter?"

"Throat, burning up . . . stomach! Oh my God, 'spoisoned!"

"It can't be . . ."

"Louis, found that clipping, had to get me before I got . . ."

He slumped to the floor, dropping the bottle and smashing it, and gripping his throat with both hands, eyes starting from their sockets as if thumbed from behind.

"Let me help you . . ."

"Oh, God, dying! Dying! Bastard!" Clutching her arm, he pulled her down to him. "You, get out now!"

"I can't get over the wall!"

"The coach is out there waiting for Otto to open the gates, bring in the horses, hitch up. Get out of here, hide in the coach!"

"What about you?"

"You can't do anything, nobody . . ."

He fell forward headfirst into the puddle of poisoned rum, his forehead cracking loudly against the stone floor. But he felt no pain, his eyes having climbed up their sockets and death stopping his heart before he struck the floor. She hesitated a moment, then fled the room, running up the stairs, pausing at the door to listen and easing it open slowly.

She would have to make her way clear across the house to the front door and outside without being seen. At least she would have to try. Starting out as quietly as she could, she got as far as the dining room and again pausing to listen, heard muffled voices floating down the main staircase to the foyer beyond and back to her. Maartens and Alma. That accounted for two of them. Where were the other two?

A chilling thought crossed her mind. If she were lucky, if no one saw her and she made it to the front door and to the coach outside, what on earth would she do if Otto was already out there hitching up his horses? She knew what he'd do, catch her and bring her screaming back, either that or finish her then and there. By now one thing was certain, her continued efforts to get away had exhausted their collective patience and any one of them would probably just as soon do away with her on the spot as bring her back to the house a third time.

Slowly she made her way through the dining room into the living room within sight of the foyer and the front door. Maartens' and Alma's voices were louder now and no longer muffled as if they were standing just at the top of the stairs, from where they could easily look down and see her approaching the door.

But she couldn't stay where she was, she'd have to take the chance. One glance turned up a penny's worth of luck; the door was unbolted, one quick pull and it would open.

Staying close to the staircase, concealing herself under the railing, she edged toward the door. Suddenly she froze; heavy footsteps were starting down the stairs directly above her. Then, as suddenly as they began they stopped and started moving back up the stairs again. Taking a deep breath, she raced forward, her feet stinging in her shoes, the half-healed blisters making their painful presence felt for the first time since she'd been brought back to the house. Reaching the door, pulling it open, she ran outside.

There stood the coach, hearselike and ominous-looking set against the darkening sky, its shafts empty, their ends resting on the semicircular gravel path. The gates beyond stood partially open and over the wall on the left horses whinnied. Otto was getting them; she had no time to lose. Running to the coach, she whipped open the door and climbed in. Under each seat there was space enough to squeeze well under out of sight. Crawling under the forward seat, she pushed as far back as she could against the paneling and, wrapping her skirt tightly about her legs, held her breath. It would be dark in fifteen or twenty minutes. If the coach didn't leave till then whoever boarded it for the ride to Harwich or Brunswick or wherever might not see her. If her luck continued there might not even be any passengers, Otto riding in alone up on top completely oblivious of his stowaway.

What would she do at the other end? That shouldn't be any problem. When he, they got where they were going Otto would tie up the team and they'd leave the coach. That would be the chance she needed. Traveling that far in her imagination it suddenly occurred to her that she didn't have a single penny on her, in itself preposterous when she remembered that she'd rowed no less than twenty thousand dollars from the cave to shore totally unaware of the good turn she would be doing Mary Elizabeth MacIntosh's "wee lad" the following morning.

She did have her return ticket, however. She'd go hungry all the way to Philadelphia, but that was an inconvenience of minor significance in the face of all she'd already endured.

She could hear Otto now, his horses snorting, hooves

clopping on gravel unrhythmically. The coach jolted and jolted again as he backed the team into the shafts and fastened their harnesses. Silence, broken only by the occasional snorting of one or another horse. Then the sound of the gate whining as he opened it all the way. Otto mounted his seat, snapped the reins—the loveliest sound she could imagine—and away they went.

She was tempted to come out from under the seat and sit on it properly, but hesitated to do so for fear that for whatever reason Otto might glance down inside the coach, in the way that most people walking down a lonely street at night snatch a quick look over their shoulder to make sure they're not being followed.

The coach jounced along uncomfortably, the top of her head striking against the side panel despite her efforts to keep it from doing so. What a blessing, to be able to ride to freedom instead of running away on her gradually healing feet. She prayed that he was headed for Brunswick, it would make it all so much easier. She could get out, get to the station and wait for the first train, even if it meant sitting beside that smelly stove till morning. Still, maybe that wouldn't be sensible at all; once Maartens found her missing he'd have to assume that she'd go directly to the station. Or would he think she'd go to the police? Whatever he thought she'd decide what to do when the journey was over and she was away from Otto and the coach.

The coach continued bouncing along, Otto holding the horses at a moderate pace. She guessed that they'd traveled no more than a mile when suddenly she heard the sound of strange hooves rapidly becoming louder. A single horse came galloping up alongside and Otto slowed and stopped. The newcomer spoke and to her horror she recognized the voice immediately.

"Get around the other side, I'll stay on this side. Other side, the door!"

Charles!

The utter futility of her situation came home to her with the suddenness of a slap on the cheek. It was useless. Getting out from under the seat, she smoothed the wrinkles out of her skirt as well as she could and, opening the door, exited the coach with an exaggeratedly imperious air, chin high, back straight, eyes boring into Charles'.

He laughed at her, and it was all she could do to keep from lunging at him and pounding him with her fists. He reached for her hand to help her down, but she ignored it and stepped down without any assistance.

"Now, there's a coincidence. I got to the house just seconds after you two left. Your host, Dr. Maartens, was very upset. Why on earth did you do such a thing?"

She glared at him. "I have nothing to say to you."

"Why did you kill poor Devereaux?"

She gasped. "Maartens told you that? He's a liar as well as a murderer!"

"But if you didn't do it, why run away?"

"You hypocrite! You disgusting, two-faced . . . What a fool I was to trust you, to believe your foul lies!"

"Get inside, we'll ride back together," he said, tying his reins to the rear of the coach.

"I prefer privacy, thank you. You can ride with Otto."

"Get in!"

She got in and he followed. Otto turned the coach around and they started back the way they'd come. She sat staring at him, her eyes filled with loathing. More than anything in the world she wanted to scratch his eyes out.

"You amaze me, Charles, you really do."

"How flattering."

"Don't be flattered. If anything I think you're far worse than any of them, even Maartens. You must love money very much to be able to watch them do away with me without batting an eye."

"You're wrong, it's been bothering me ever since Maartens decided it had to be done. I never planned on this. I've never killed anybody and I never will."

"How noble. Wouldn't hurt a fly, would you, but you wouldn't hesitate to let Maartens do as he pleases."

"It's his decision, not mine. Believe me, if there was anything I could do . . ."

"You've done quite enough, thank you."

They rode a ways in silence and, if anything, the urge to attack his eyes strengthened itself.

"I'm curious," she said at length, "whatever possessed you to get involved with him in the first place? Or is that too simple a question, like why does one swine choose to wallow in the same mudhole with another?"

"I wallow for money, what else? What would you say if I told you that cooperating with Hendrik I can make as much in three days as the hospital pays me for a whole year!"

"You lucky fellow. You'd sell your soul for a dollar, wouldn't you?"

"Not quite that cheaply, I'm afraid. First off I'd have to check the going price for souls."

"Very funny. You must be proud of yourself."

"Let's say I'm well satisfied."

"You realize, of course, it's all over. Devereaux's dead and the old woman; Maartens is ready to leave . . . You're going to be left high and dry. What do you plan to do when the birds fly away?"

"That's easy, go back to business as usual. The only difference between before and after is that I'll be quite a few thousand richer."

"And what will you do with it, build a hospital for crippled waifs?"

"Now you're being funny. No, not funny, ridiculous. Why is it naive little girls like you all seem to think that we healers are more than mortals, gifted saints with scalpels surviving handily on the adulation of the masses and never needing anything as dirty as money? Alison, my love, you can't believe the difference this money is going to make in the way I live . . ."

"That won't be the real difference. The real difference is I'm alive now and when they leave I'll be dead, thanks to my charming cousin. All the money in the world won't help you live with that on your conscience!"

"Conscience, me? Little girl, my conscience doesn't enter into it, not for a second. It's a simple case of self-preservation. I have an absolute horror of ropes with nooses at the end. I don't intend to hang for what I've done. I haven't committed a hanging offense, but if you live and they catch me, they'll string me higher than a Christmas goose. And who but you would be the one to blame for it, which when you think about it would put me squarely on your conscience. Good God, I'm actually doing you a favor. If you'd stayed overnight at the Speedwell like any sensible person, if you hadn't started out and ended up at Barringer House you wouldn't have blundered into things! All our wheels would have continued rolling smoothly, Devereaux would be alive and Hendrik wouldn't have a murder charge hanging over his head."

"It's not the first one."

"I haven't the slightest interest in his past experiences. The point is, he could hang for the Devereaux episode, the least that can happen is this entire affair would open like a flower. And swallow us up! You're to blame. You got yourself into this, not me. You pay the piper, not Maartens, not any of us."

"You're marvelous, Charles. And to think I considered you a man. But you're the furthest thing from a real man. You've allowed this whole affair to emasculate you completely. Without the slightest hesitation you defer to the will of a madman because you haven't the courage to cross him. Well, whether I live or die, one day the law'll catch up with you and when it does you'll be done for. A man might battle back and survive, but not you. All because you've let him drain every last drop of self-respect, sincerity and honesty out of you. And you won't have the strength or the heart to stand up and defend yourself, you pitiful excuse for a human being!"

8

They returned to Barringer House, Otto turning in through the gate, letting them out, putting Charles' horse in for the night and leaving, his own horses clattering away at a brisk gallop. Charles escorted her up the gravel way to the door, holding her elbow firmly.

"You know why he poisoned Devereaux."

"That's between the two of them, it doesn't concern you or me."

"My error. You have a unique talent, Charles . . . the ostrich with his head in the sand, anything you don't like, anything that displeases or embarrasses you, you merely close your eyes and away it goes. Devereaux's murder, mine . . . no concern of yours, are they? The only trouble with that attitude is you might be making a mistake. He killed Devereaux over an insignificant newspaper clipping. If it takes as little as that to set him off, you could be in a bit of danger yourself."

"Not such an insignificant newspaper clipping. The mere fact that he hung onto the thing told Hendrik all he needed to know about Devereaux's loyalty. You see, when somebody's bent on making life difficult for another, the object of their disaffection does himself a great disservice if he neglects to get in the first blow. Why defend when you can attack?"

"Why, indeed? Such an honorable fraternity you people

are. I'm surprised you don't all carry knives and sleep with one eye open."

Inside the door, noting that only Maartens was there to welcome them back, she seized the initiative, deciding on the spot that at this point she had little left to lose. Breaking free of Charles' grip, she ran past the astonished Maartens toward the sea cliff end of the house.

"Stop her!" roared the older man.

Through the living room she ran, into the dining room past a startled Alma. Spurred by desperation, slamming doors behind her as she ran, she reached the entrance to the kitchen and avoiding it, knowing that once inside she'd find herself trapped, she turned to the right, racing down a narrow hallway to the door at the end, running into the room, locking and bolting the door behind her.

It was Maartens' lab, crammed with equipment, tables filled with it and shelves with labeled bottles and flasks of every description. The acrid odor of ammonia combined with chemicals unfamiliar to her reached her nostrils. She looked about. Against the far wall stood a wheeled table, a sheet draped over it reaching all the way to the floor. Stretched out on the table was the shrouded corpse of the old woman. There was no mistaking that face, even in death. Maartens and Charles came up to the door and began pounding it, demanding she open it.

"Alma, Alma!" roared Maartens. "Get my pistol in the top drawer! Hurry!"

"Alison, don't be a fool!" yelled Charles.

Why waste her breath on either of them? This was her last chance and she was determined to make the most of it. Seizing the largest table by one leg, she dragged it up to the door, tipping it over, sending everything on it crashing to the floor. Then she wedged the edge of the top under the knob. This done, she snatched up everything that looked as if it might burn and piling it against the table, lit a friction match from a box beside a Bunsen burner, ignited the burner and tossed it at the pile, half expecting an horrendous explosion to result.

Flames leaped from the pile heaped up against the table, a curtain of fire concealing the door behind. She ran to the other end of the room to the door leading to the east wing of the house. Pulling it open, she left it that way and going to the twin sinks beside the corpse of the old lady, tore a strip from the hem of her skirt, wet it under the tap and, concealing herself under the wheeled table behind the sheet, held the dampened cloth against her nose and mouth.

Shots sounded above the crackling flames, slamming into the lock and bolt. Then the door was pushed from the other side. Charles kicked through the opening, dislodging the table barring the way from under the doorknob. It crashed to the floor upside down, scattering fire about. Through the sheet she could see Charles fling the door wide.

"The back way!" shouted Maartens.

They dashed in yelling loudly, running through the room and out the back door, Alma following a few steps behind.

Emerging from her hiding place, she moved to the open front door and out into the hallway. Starting back the way she had come, she ran through the dining and living rooms into the foyer and out of the house.

The gates stood wide. She ran out, turning left down the road paralleling the direction she had taken three nights earlier, following the shoreline down the cliff.

But she did not stick to the road for long. They would be on her trail very soon, probably following on horseback. On the road she would be helpless; her only chance lay in getting across the fields into the spreading stand of pines a half mile or so to her right. Her feet did not hurt nearly as much as she'd feared they would, but whether they hurt or not she was in no frame of mind to permit anything as inconsequential as a little discomfort to slow her down.

If she were lucky, if she managed to reach the trees before they caught sight of her, she might count herself reasonably safe, although as she thought about it, running along through the waist-high grass, she concluded that Maartens and Charles were too intelligent not to anticipate such an obvious strategy, particularly when they failed to spot her on the road or near it. They would know that she wouldn't head for the shoreline. Without a boat she'd be too easily trapped between them and the sea. Maartens had a gun; in the foul mood she'd managed to put him in he'd probably use it. Why bring her back to Barringer House alive? She'd promise far less future annoyance with a bullet or two in her!

There were three or four other houses in the immediate area in addition to Barringer House and no sooner had this thought crossed her mind, having by this time reached the pines and passed through them, than she saw a house less than a hundred yards away, almost directly in front of her.

A one-story building hugging the earth, its single chimney sent a slender column of gray-white smoke heavenward. The surrounding fence was undergoing repairs at its near corners and by the gate. To the right, on the verge of exhausting its ability to remain upright, stood a large, homely-looking barn.

Swinging the front gate wide, she passed through, making her way up the path to the door. The knocker was a horseshoe, flattened by too many miles and now adapted to the task of announcing visitors. Grasping it, she hesitated, then rapped loudly.

No sound came from within and after waiting a full minute, while she considered that she might be stepping from the frying pan into the fire, she rapped again. It was not yet eight o'clock, but Maine farmers, she guessed, retired much earlier than Philadelphians. At that, how many of the latter arose at dawn? Presently, a glimmer of light crossed the window left of the door, a bolt sounded and the door eased open. An oil lamp greeted her, behind it a middle-aged woman in night clothes. Her hair hanging loosely about her shoulders was going to gray and her face supporting it impressed Alison as that rare sort that prides itself on looking older than it actually is. It is almost as if such individuals believe that the sooner one gets to the late years, the sooner one comes by the dignity and respect to which old people are entitled and so they hasten to their seniority.

"Who . . . what do you want?"

"My name is Alison Collier. May I come in, please?"

She explained hurriedly, now and then casting an apprehensive glance back over her shoulder.

The woman looked shocked and confused at the same time, her forehead wrinkling and the corners of her mouth turning down.

"Jenny, who is it?" asked a man's voice behind her. His hand came around the door, pulling it all the way open. It was Braden Gilyard! Nightshirt, nightcap, and smile of recognition, the most welcome sight imaginable!

"Well, well, look who's here, Hagar herself! And still wandering about the countryside in the dead of night! Well, don't stand there, my dear, come in, come in!"

The woman stepped aside and Alison entered. The front room was warm and comfortable-looking, lived in and obviously enjoyed, from its antimacassars draped over the shabby chairs to the immense rag rug concealing most of the otherwise bare floor to the spinning wheel, its distaff halfway through a bolt of yarn.

But there was nevertheless an air of poverty about the place, a first impression one got that the harvest had been poor, that money was short, and continued survival for those who lived in this house touch and go.

She poured out her story, the words tumbling one upon the other, relating essentials only and emphasizing the danger confronting her.

"But why are these fellows after you, what did you do to them?" asked Gilyard.

"Nothing, believe me. One of them killed one of the others, a Dr. Devereaux. Just my luck I was a witness. This Maartens, this other doctor, the one who did the killing, is convinced I'll report him to the police. He has to stop me any way he can . . ."

"All these people be living at Barringer House?" asked Mrs. Gilyard. "Law, I didn't know no one was there."

"They're scouring the area, I'm sure. They'll be here any minute. I beg you, don't give me away!"

"Needn't worry about that," said Gilyard reassuringly. "Up into the attic with you and stay out of sight. And mind you don't make a move. They'll hear the boards creakin' and know you're up there . . ."

They hurried her past the fireplace over which a lovely oval-shaped mirror in a gilded wooden frame reflected the interior of the house. Up a crudely fashioned stairway she climbed to the attic. Reaching the top and pulling herself through the square opening, she turned about and peered down.

"Slide the trapdoor over," ordered Gilyard. "Find a spot and stay there. And don't creak the boards!"

"Hisst!" Mrs. Gilyard touched her lips with her finger.

Silence and out of it came the sound of galloping, closer, closer, two horses pulling up and then an insistent rapping of the knocker, a singular sound that chilled her to the bone. Having fixed the trapdoor in place over the makeshift stairway, she had crawled through the stuffy darkness toward the front of the house between baskets, barrels and boxes and found a spot directly over the center of the front room where lying face down, she was able to peer through a quarter-inch space between boards and see the rag rug below and the tops of the heads of both Gilyards.

"Open the door!" exclaimed a muffled voice.

Holding her breath, she watched as Mrs. Gilyard smoothed her nightdress, straightened her hair about her shoulders and, moving lamp in hand to the door, unbolted and opened it.

Gilyard came up behind her, easing her to one side and confronting Charles and Dr. Maartens.

"Do forgive us for intruding on you at this hour," said Maartens unctuously. "I am Dr. Hendrik Maartens and this is my colleague, Dr. Charles Collier of the East Cumberland County Hospital. We're here to warn you . . ."

"About what?" asked Gilyard guardedly.

"A young woman has escaped from the hospital. She's hopelessly insane. The poor demented creature . . . she's already killed one of the staff and if we don't catch her she'll probably kill again."

"She's extremely dangerous," said Charles.

"Have you seen her, or seen anything suspicious around here tonight?" asked Maartens.

"Nothin'," said Gilyard flatly, "we were just about to go to bed."

"Brown hair, medium height, early twenties," interjected

Charles, "and she may have a knife. If she does, she won't hesitate to use it. She has already . . ."

"We've been combing the countryside," said Maartens, "we must find her, at all costs. There's a substantial reward, a thousand dollars to anyone with information leading to her apprehension."

"A thousand dollars?" Mrs. Gilyard gasped and flashed a quick look at her husband.

"No questions asked," added Charles.

Maartens stared at the woman and his right hand went to his inside jacket pocket. Taking out his wallet, he revealed a thick handful of bills.

"I ask you again, have you seen her? Have you any idea where she may be?"

"We haven't seen hide nor hair of a soul all day," said Gilyard. "You're the first."

Charles looked around the room. "This place is the only one in the neighborhood showing a light," he said.

"And that'll be out in a trice. It's late and as you can see we're ready for bed."

"Of course. Again, we apologize for intruding, but this poor unfortunate girl simply must be found. Until she's put away, no one is safe. If you don't mind, if it's not too inconvenient, we would like to search the house. She may have sneaked in the back door without your knowing."

"Nobody's sneaked in here," said Gilyard, stepping aside and gesturing, "see for yourself. Wait . . ."

Starting forward, Charles stopped abruptly.

"What is it?"

"The barn," said Gilyard, "she could be hidin' in the barn!"

Maartens and Charles exchanged glances. "May we look?" asked the older man.

"Of course. You find her there and you'll give us a thousand dollars?" asked Gilyard.

"Cash in hand," said Maartens.

Gilyard seized the lamp from his wife. "I'll take you, we'll all three look. I'll bet a good dog she's hidin' in the hay. Come, hurry . . . if she heard your husses, she may have got frightened and made off!"

Charles and Maartens followed him out the door, Mrs. Gilyard closing it after them.

"A thousand dollars, all the money in the world," she said bitterly, shaking her head, and looked up at the rafters.

Ten minutes later, hooves sounded again, pounding the ground and galloping off into the night. Then Gilyard came back into the house.

"All clear, miss," he said, raising his voice. She came back down the attic steps.

They sat at a homemade table, Gilyard across from her, his wife at her left, the woman studying her strangely as if looking for signs of irrational behavior, hoping to find them, thought Alison, wanting Maartens' money so much she could hardly control herself.

She would have to get out of there as soon as possible, preferably before dawn, although where she would go and how she'd be able to keep clear of Charles and Maartens was another matter.

"Where would you go?" Gilyard asked when she suggested leaving.

She sighed and smiled at him wanly. "Perhaps it's only fair that I tell you the whole story, from beginning to end."

"We'll listen, if it be the truth you tell us," said Mrs. Gilyard archly.

"It's the truth, all right, but I must warn you that you'll find it dreadfully hard to believe. If our situations were reversed and you were to tell it to me, I could find it very easy to doubt every word. But it's no lie, no part of it."

She began with her arrival in Brunswick and took them all the way up to her first attempt at escape from Barringer House. Then Mrs. Gilyard interrupted, shooting to her feet and pointing out the window.

"Heaven preserve us, look!"

All three gathered at the window. The group of pines which separated the Gilyards' land from the field beyond and the road beyond that ended less than two hundred yards from the corner of the fence. To the left of the last tree in the near distance a sheet of flame leaped high into the sky.

"It's Barringer House!" exclaimed Gilyard.

Alison stared in shock and disbelief. The flames rose a hundred feet in the air, blending into a single enormous tongue, as if hell itself imprisoned in the core of the earth had burned a passage up through it, bursting through the surface and challenging the heavens with its awesome fury! Slicing upward through the blackness of the night, the fire swelled, becoming larger as she watched transfixed by the sight. Then turning away, closing her eyes, she imagined the living room, its drapes blazing up and the walls igniting while Captain Barringer and his love continued to stare at each other through the billowing smoke and flames, determinedly ignoring the carnage engulfing them even as they were attacked and consumed and reduced to ashes.

She hoped that Alma and Otto, if by now he had returned, and Nurse Raphael had been able to get out safely before the fire got out of hand. Her conscience twinged at the thought that any of them might have been trapped inside, she having started it.

She concluded her story, noting as she did that doubt

still lingered in Mrs. Gilyard's eyes. All three went to bed, Alison being shown to a child's bed in the corner of the small room at the rear of the house. Evidently, the Gilyards had had a child who, whatever the reason, was no longer with them.

They bade her good night with his assurance that he would take her to the Brunswick station the following morning and stay with her until she boarded her train for home.

"You're safe with us, my dear, till you're on your way," he said.

She lay in the small bed staring at the ceiling, afraid to fall asleep lest Charles and Maartens return and find her, confront her in the bed and seize her before she could make it to the door. Mrs. Gilyard wanted the money passionately, it was written all over the woman's face. And the fact that she had reluctantly deferred to her husband's judgment and held her peace while Charles and Maartens were there failed to comfort Alison. It was possible that at that very moment the two of them lay in bed discussing the situation, she alternately pleading and insisting that he change his mind, ride out, find "those two" and turn "her" over to them like so much misplaced baggage and he gradually coming around to her view.

A thousand dollars after all was a fortune to the Gilyards in the world, hard-working people with so little to show for their labor, and in such obvious need. Such a sum might well be the difference between surviving and going under in the face of winter coming on the heels of a lean harvest. A harsh and forbidding land, the state of Maine, demanding and challenging and no Eden for those who sought to wrest a living from its resources.

But for all her pessimism regarding Mrs. Gilyard she

could not let go of the conviction that Mr. Gilyard was on her side, that he had accepted her every word as gospel and that the thousand dollar inducement to give her away tempted him not at all, he being the sort whose principles could never be compromised by any amount of money, particularly in the form of a bribe.

A pity some of the man's character couldn't rub off on dear Charles.

She sneezed twice, sufficient to remind her that the cold she had contracted earlier was still with her, although very slight. She fell asleep in spite of her fear of doing so, the events of the evening having exhausted her.

Shortly after sun-up she was awakened by the sound of a horse outside her window. Fear struck at her heart, her first thought being that Charles and Maartens had returned, summoned by the Gilyards.

But it was neither of them, only Gilyard himself readying his wagon. He came to the window motioning her to open it.

"I'm takin' Dolly in to Brunswick to find out when your train will be leavin'. When I get back we'll wait till an hour afore it goes, then I'll take you in. Shouldn't be waitin' 'round that station any long time. It's too chancy, those two may still be out lookin' for you."

"Mr. Gilyard, I can't tell you how much I appreciate all you've done for me."

"Nonsense, girl, it's no more than what any human bein' should do for any other. Get yourself up now and dressed. Jen'll fix you breakfast. I've told her to lock the door and keep it locked while I'm gone. Neither of you is to open it to a soul. And if anyone comes prowlin' about you're to get up into the attic like you did before and stay there till I get back."

"I will."

Hitching up his horse, he drove off. Mrs. Gilyard knocked at the door and invited her to breakfast, fresh eggs, delicious homemade bread and sweet milk. Evidently, from her manner and her tone, the woman had changed her mind about weighing Maartens' offer against the safety of her uninvited guest. Or more likely her husband had changed her mind for her, for she was unusually warm and friendly.

"Did you sleep well, dear?"

"Very well, thank you."

Mrs. Gilyard apologized for the smallness of the bed, explaining that it had been their daughter's. Her voice took on an edge of sadness and a far-away look came into her eyes.

"Her name were Rosemary, my mother's name. Poor little tyke died of the pneumonia, only nine years in this world." She studied Alison. "If she'd lived she'd be just about your age. She'd look like you, too, same coloring, same eyes and a smile sweet as your own. But she's dead, our Rosemary . . . I thought when it happened 'twould kill Braden, he loved her so. Adored her. Never called her by her rightful name; she was always Angel to him. My Angel, he'd say, Angel this, Angel that. And now she be with the angels . . ."

"I'm very sorry."

"The Lord giveth, the Lord taketh away. Praise be the Lord. Eat all you please, your cheeks be pinched and your color's wan, you need a good meal."

They ate in silence until Alison asked about the fire.

"Barringer House be burned to the ground," said the older woman. "Come look out the window."

They went to the window. Where the house had stood dominating the cliff overlooking the sea were now only two or three charred beams poking up above the blackened walls.

"I wonder if the people got out alive?" asked Alison.

"Who knows? As for the house, good riddance I say. It be an evil place. Barringer be an evil man, so they say. I've the good fortune never to have crossed his path."

A knock sounded at the door and Alison started, her hand going to her throat in fear, Mrs. Gilyard glanced at her and taking her by the hand, walked toward the door. Again a knock.

"Who's there?"

"Open the door, please, I must speak with you. It's a matter of life and death."

"Who are you?"

That voice, it was familiar to Alison, but she could not place it immediately. Then it came to her.

"My name is Hampton."

"Don't open it," she whispered hoarsely, "don't let him in! He's one of them. It's a trick, they've sent him to get me because they think I trust him. He's as bad as the other two, please don't let him in!"

"Go away," said Mrs. Gilyard firmly.

"Open the door, please. I must speak with you!"

Like a sudden illness striking, fear rose up inside her, filling her throat and flooding her mind. Panicking, she turned and ran back through the house and out the door, Mrs. Gilyard's voice ringing in her ears.

She started across the field behind the house, dodging between corn shocks, stumbling, falling once, picking herself up and continuing her flight.

"Alison!" He had seen her and was coming after her across the field, calling her name again and again and closing the gap between them.

She must get away! She would die rather than let him catch her!

"Alison, stop!"

She ran and ran until at length her lungs surrendered, air refusing to enter them, her legs turning to jelly and no longer able to support her. She collapsed at the edge of a narrow road twisting down a hill into the morning mist. Now she could hear his footsteps coming closer.

"Alison . . ."

He came running up beside her, bending to help her to her feet.

"Don't touch me!"

9

He held her in his arms, smiling down at her. Her heart sank and with her last remaining strength she began beating his chest with her fists.

"Alison, Alison, it's all right, I won't hurt you . . ."

"They sent you!"

"No, no, no . . ." He cradled her head against his chest and stroked her hair tenderly, his voice soothing, comforting. "It's all over for all of them. The police have rounded them up."

"I don't understand . . ."

"I don't myself, except that the woman, the nurse . . ."

"Raphael!"

"She went to the authorities in Brunswick sometime last night and told them the entire story."

Understanding brightened her eyes and she smiled. "Yes, yes, of course. She must have been furious with Maartens for what he did to Devereaux."

"I don't know anything about that."

"She'd have to have her vengeance, and as quickly as she could, even if it means sticking her own neck in the noose!"

He sobered. "Charles is involved."

"I know . . ."

"I'm sorry."

"Don't be. He deserves everything that's coming to him. But tell me, how in the world did you find me? How did you know?" Sitting up, she stared at him quizzically.

"I put two and two together, dozens of twos. I got back from Boston fairly late last evening and Charles wasn't around. I had no idea you'd been in the hospital earlier in the week until one of the nurses mentioned it. I overheard her talking with the head nurse."

"MacIntosh."

"Yes. She was wondering why you'd vanished so suddenly, where you'd gone. Naturally, my curiosity was aroused. When we couldn't find you in the wreckage of Burgess' coach and we went looking for you, Charles and I both assumed . . . well, frankly neither of us knew what to assume."

"What else did she tell you?"

"She said you'd come to the hospital and that Charles was taking care of you, that she didn't know anything about you except that you and he were cousins. She told me how you two had talked, how she took care of your feet and that she'd given you something to make you sleep, on his orders."

"But how did you figure out where I was?"

"Patience . . . she told me that you must have taken your sleeping draught sometime between nine and nine-fifteen because when she went into the room to check on you you were dead to the world."

"Please . . . don't use that word!"

"Sorry. You looked uncomfortable and she was arranging your pillow when you started talking in your sleep."

"That's ridiculous, I never talk in my sleep."

"You did that night, and lucky for you. Anyway, MacIntosh said she couldn't understand most of what you were saying except over and over again you kept repeating Barringer House, as if you were deathly afraid of the place. Then I remembered that that was one of the places Charles and I stopped by to inquire about you after we found the wrecked coach. The woman who came to the door denied you were there and we went away. But I got to thinking that since you're a stranger around here the only possible way you'd know about Barringer House and be able to describe the place as you did talking in your sleep would be if you'd actually been there. Now, the condition you'd arrived at the hospital in suggested you'd run away from some place. I figured Barringer House."

"What did you think when MacIntosh told you I'd disappeared a second time?"

"Only that you had a strange habit of turning up missing when I wanted most to see you. But let me go on. Since Charles wasn't at the hospital and nobody seemed to know where he was I checked his room, found he wasn't there either, so having no other lead I started out for Barringer House hoping that's where the two of you were. By the time I got a horse and gig and got within sight of the place . . ."

"It was on fire, of course!"

"Burning like the end of the world. I can tell you my heart sank, especially after telling myself all the way out from Harwich that you were there. I drove like the wind but by the time I got there it was an absolute inferno. The gates had collapsed and you could see inside the grounds. There wasn't a soul around, no sign of anyone in the ashes when the fire died out, no sign of any coach or horses, nothing."

"Charles and Maartens were out looking for me and the other three must have gotten away. I'm glad, it was I who started the fire."

"You?"

Together they walked slowly back toward the house and she told him the whole story beginning with the accident involving Burgess' coach. Gene listened raptly, and his reaction was one she was becoming used to:

"Incredible!"

"What will they do with them?"

"It's hard to say. They'll be brought to trial, of course. It seems a fairly complicated mess, the law's going to have to get all the knots untied. You'll probably be called to testify."

"No, thank you!"

"They'll need you. They won't have anybody to back up the nurse's story. And after all you've been through they'll take what you tell them as the unvarnished truth. You're the only objective witness they'll have."

"I'm not interested. Tell me the rest, what made you come here?"

"I drove back to town in the dead of night, checked Charles' place a second time, then went back to the hospital. I have a room there where I sometimes sleep over when I work late. I planned on getting up early and taking the entire day to look for you. To be honest, I was upset with myself. I'd let Charles follow up on everything, taking it for granted that he could handle things . . ."

"What could you do, you were out of town?"

"I know, but I never should have gone."

"I wonder when you couldn't find me last night that you didn't think I'd gotten on a train and gone back to Philadelphia."

"I thought of that, just before I fell asleep. I even imagined the reason I couldn't find Charles was that he'd decided to go with you. What bothered me about that was that he hadn't seen fit to tell anybody at the hospital. Staff doctors just don't walk out without letting the office know where they're going and how long they'll be away. Then the whole mystery cleared up in the wink of an eye."

"How?"

"I was sleeping in my room when Lawrence Pyle, one of the orderlies, came in and woke me. He'd gotten word that Charles had been arrested with the others and he wanted to know what we should do. What he expected us to do in the middle of the night I'll never know. My first impulse was to go to the police station, get in to see Charles, see if I might do anything for him and ask him where you were. At that point, you see, I didn't know any of the details . . . nothing. But while I was getting dressed Pyle and I both got word on why Charles had been taken in. Not the whole story, mind you, but enough to convince me that something unusual had been going on at Barringer House while I was in Boston, and that he was in on it. You had already run away from there once, that much I'd guessed from what MacIntosh told me. And once I knew that he was mixed up in the thing, I figured it could have been he who'd taken you back to the house. And since they were out looking for you, you must have gotten away from them a second time, so it was possible you were hiding somewhere around the area. I got out the gig I'd used earlier and started scouting around. Gilyard's house was the third one I went to, the second one I nearly got my head shot off."

"Oh, Lord . . ."

He stopped short and stared. "What am I doing? A fine friend I am, you've been through all this, you're on the verge of collapse and here I am walking you back all this way. Let me carry you . . ."

"Nonsense. Don't worry about me, I've plenty of time to collapse on the train. Right now I'm so stirred up by what's happened I could practically run to town."

"I'll take you back in the gig. We'll find out about your train. I expect you'll want to get home as quickly as you can."

"I should, Gene."

"Of course. Strange, isn't it?"

"What?"

"We never do see each other for more than a few minutes at a time. Maybe when all this is cleared up I could take some time off . . ."

"And come visit me in Philadelphia. I'd like that."

"Would you?"

"Very much."

"I've never been south of Boston. You'd have to lead me around by the hand."

"I'd like that, too."

By this time they had crossed the field and were nearing the house. There was no sign of Dolly and the wagon or Dolly's owner, but Mrs. Gilyard spied them coming and opened the back door.

"Be you all right, Alison?" she asked worriedly.

"Never better."

"You certain? It's mighty strange. He comes to the door and you run off lickity split, frightened out of your wits by him. Now you come back hanging onto his arm." She glared at Gene as she continued talking to Alison. "If I didn't know better I'd think he was the Devil himself cast a spell over you. He's red enough for Old Scratch!"

Alison laughed and Gene sighed mock dejection.

"We'll be going now. I'm riding back with Mr. Hampton here."

"You'll not be waiting for Braden?"

"There's no need. Besides, I've inconvenienced him too much already. Please tell him that I thank him, and thank you for all you've done. When I get home I'll write you both a letter."

The woman continued staring at Gene. "I hope you know what you're doing."

"She does," said Gene flatly.

Mrs. Gilyard shrugged. Her features relaxed into a smile, she waved as if tossing them off, and retreated into the house. They walked around to the front and through the gate and Gene helped her up onto the seat. Untying his horse, he sat beside her, reins in hand.

"Will you do something for me?" she asked as she turned to respond to Mrs. Gilyard's parting wave from the front doorway.

"Name it."

"Can you drive past the house?"

"Barringer House?"

She nodded. "It's the last look I'll ever get of it."

"I'm afraid there's not much to see."

"Please."

"If you want."

He slapped the horse's flanks with a quick snap of the reins and it doubled its pace. Within minutes they came up to what remained of Captain Barringer's ill-fated residence. The gates were open, but they might better have been closed, locked and blocking the sight of the debacle within.

The house had been reduced to a low-lying heap of rubble, the wind swirling over the walls scooping up ashes and flinging them over the cliff, invisible hands tossing the bones of the house into the sea below.

She pictured clearly each of the rooms in relationship to the others, recalling the ceremony, the lonely venison dinner, the kitchen, the laboratory and most of all her bedroom perched on the edge of the cliff, the very floor of heaven.

This shapeless mass spread from one wall to the other, covering and concealing all the evil fantasies come to life which she had experienced and endured, this hive of maleficence that was no more, reduced to nothingness by a fate that could ill accept its existence in the first place. The whole dreary aspect infused her with a strange feeling, a reaction akin to but not quite pity.

"What are you thinking about?" he asked.

"It sounds silly, I suppose, but I almost feel sorry for it."

"The house itself?"

She nodded. "It was so abused, victimized, made to suffer and die despised and damned. Everyone who used it cared only for themselves and their twisted ambitions. A house is so helpless, it can't choose those who live in it any more than a dog can choose its master."

"Bad people living in good houses, is that it?"

"I am sorry I burned it down. I certainly had no intention . . ."

"They didn't give you much choice."

"It's a crime just the same."

"Alison, believe me, most people around these parts who know Barringer House and its history will be relieved to see it gone. I wouldn't be surprised if the men got together and shoveled every last trace of it over the cliff into the sea, although what the sharks have done to deserve that I can't say. Seen enough?"

"Yes."

"The cemetery's just up the way. Do you want to stop by before we head back?"

They climbed the hill to her father's grave and stood over it, gazing down in silence. Then she lifted her eyes and looked at him.

"I wish there were some wildflowers . . ."

"I'll get some flowers out here," he said.

They returned to the gig and started for Brunswick. Within sight of town, Braden Gilyard appeared coming from the opposite direction. Recognizing her, he waved and pulled up beside them. She introduced Gene and explained to the older man.

"Your train leaves a few minutes after nine o'clock," said Gilyard. "You got your ticket?"

"Yes. Mr. Gilyard, Braden, thank you so much for all you've done for me."

"Pleasure. Take good care of her, young fellow. And, Hagar, when you come back one day, come visit us."

"I will."

"Promise." He smiled, waved and drove off.

"Hagar?" asked Gene.

"Hagar in the wilderness. The Bible," she said and explained.

The remainder of the way, through town to the other side, he resisted the urge to break into her thoughts, for which she was grateful. He was such a sensitive man, she thought, knowing instinctively when to talk and when to be silent, one of his so many admirable qualities. She studied his profile out of the corner of her eye as they wheeled along. When at last they came within sight of the railroad station it was she who broke the silence.

"What is the matter with me?"

"What do you mean?"

"I want to go home, I know I should. I have a duty to, but . . ."

"I'm going with you. That's why we're stopping here now, I'll have to buy my ticket."

She brightened momentarily, just long enough to tell him that this was exactly what she hoped he'd say. Then she again lapsed into her mood.

"You can't . . ."

"Who says I can't? I can take a couple of days away from

the hospital. It won't collapse. Tomorrow's Sunday, I'll be off anyway. I'll see you safely home and come back Monday, maybe even early Tuesday. I can't let you go alone, I'm worried about you."

"Why?"

"You've been through a lot. I'm not a doctor, but I've been around hospitals long enough to see what usually happens in cases like this."

"I feel fine."

"Right now, yes, that's part relief at being snatched from the proverbial jaws and part nerves. Tonight, tomorrow the whole thing will trigger a reaction, suddenly you'll feel weak as a kitten, so exhausted you won't be able to lift your hand."

"And you want to be there to lift it for me . . ."

"Why not? I won't be in the way."

She gasped. "I never said you would be!"

"I love you, Alison. We've had no time together, and this is our chance. We can sit on the train and talk till our teeth ache."

"What did you say?"

He stopped the horse in the middle of the narrow road. "I said we can sit on the train . . ."

"You said I love you."

"I do, so very much."

She touched his cheek and gazed at him longingly, then leaning forward kissed him on the cheek. "You are so dear . . ."

"Then it's settled. Philadelphia, here we come. Oh yes, there's one more reason for my getting out of town. You don't know Mr. Butters . . ."

"Who?"

"Butters. He's not as funny as his name. Come to think

of it he's not funny at all. Bosses never are. Mr. Butters is the supervisor at the hospital. When he gets to work Monday morning he'll come roaring into my office with his mustaches waving and his neck as red as a beet. He'll refresh my memory, bluntly informing me that it was I who recommended hiring Charles."

"Mr. Butters will be worried over what people think . . . the hospital's reputation?"

"Worried is not the word, outraged is more like it. And not 'people,' it's the board of directors."

"You won't lose your job, will you?"

"Oh, no . . . I doubt if Mr. Butters will go that far. But if I gave him a day or so to cool down it might be easier on my eardrums."

"But won't he think you're running out for just that purpose?"

"I'm sure he will. He'll know, I'll know, you'll know. Nevertheless, he happens to be extremely loud and my eardrums extremely sensitive. They'll appreciate the reprieve."

He kissed her. Someone yelled behind them and both turned to look. No fewer than three carriages of varying sizes and numbers of occupants were lined up, blocked by their gig.

"If you let us past, we'll be able to see better from the other side," said a man in the last carriage and the others laughed.

Gene blushed, started the horse and they bolted away in such haste she was thrown against the back of the seat, laughing uproariously.

At the station, he bought his ticket and they stood by the gig taking in the early morning sunshine and watching the town come to life. And they sent a telegram of explanation to her mother.

"Alison, we still have almost an hour and a half before the train leaves. I really ought to go over to Harwich to the hospital and tell them I won't be in Monday."

"I was thinking about that. And there's another thing . . ."

He sobered and nodded. "We ought to go see him."

"We should. It seems wrong somehow, getting on the train and riding off without a word to him."

"I'll pop in and see if there's anything he needs."

"I'll come, too."

"If you want to. It may not be too pleasant."

They stopped at the hospital, then walked down the block and around the corner to the police station, a weather-stricken old building with a sign badly in need of repainting over its double front door. Inside, the room was shabbily furnished, a long wooden bench, a table and a few chairs, coat racks on two of the walls and a gun rack with weapons locked in place on a third. A broom stood in one corner, a small pile of sweepings beside it. They approached a uniformed officer sitting in the opposite corner diagonally across from the unfinished task, ignoring it in favor of his newspaper.

"Excuse me," said Gene, "but would it be possible for us to see one of your prisoners?"

"Which one?" The man folded his newspaper and eyed them suspiciously.

"Charles Collier," said Alison.

"Oh, him . . . he gave us a peck of trouble when they brought him in. Yelling, carrying on, I thought he'd tear the place apart. We had to put him in irons. You members of his family?"

"I'm his cousin."

"And I work with him at the hospital. Eugene Hampton."

"I don't know . . . we don't usually allow visitors, outside wives or husbands or lawyers, before prisoner's arraigned. And his lawyer's coming in . . ."

"We're leaving town, all we'd want is a couple of minutes."

The man hesitated, looking from one to the other. "Oh, all right. I'll fetch him into the visitors' room. I'll have to ask you to empty your pockets, though, sir. Not that I suspect you'd be trying to smuggle anything in to him, but that's the rule. Nothing personal, you understand. Step on over to that table."

Gene emptied his pockets under the officer's watchful eye.

"I appreciate this."

"Wait here, I'll bring him to the room, then call you both in."

He vanished.

"I've changed my mind," said Alison. "I'll wait here while you go in."

"But why?"

She shook her head. "I can't see him in chains . . ."

He placed a comforting hand on her forearm. "It's not really that, is it? It's not that you don't want to see him, it's you don't want him to see you."

"He's hurt himself enough, maybe more than he can bear. I wouldn't want him feeling embarrassment or pity for me, to add to his burden."

"I understand. I'll only be a few minutes."

"Don't tell him I'm here."

"I won't."

They sat on the wooden bench by the front door listening to the clicking of key in lock, the clanging of a metal door, and the ominous rattle of chains. Presently the officer reappeared in the doorway.

"Five minutes," he said and escorted Gene inside, coming back out and resuming his reading.

She heard Gene greet Charles and Charles respond, his tone pretended happy-go-lucky, as if he hadn't a care in the world.

"Well, well, well, my first visitor. And a sight for sore eyes if ever there was one. Sit down, Gene old fellow. I'd offer you a nip of gin, but as you can see the amenities in this lovely hostelry leave something to be desired. What do you think of my fancy restrainers, wrists and ankles both no less? Thirty pounds if they're an ounce. I feel like an overloaded galley slave!" He laughed hollowly and Alison's eyes misted.

"Is there anything I can get you?" asked Gene, "anything at all you need?"

"I don't think so. Got a good lawyer, Franklin Moore from Bath."

"He's a very good lawyer, so they say."

"Nothing but the best, although he won't have much to do. They can't do anything to me. You can't prosecute a doctor for practicing medicine now, can you?"

"I guess not."

"Bet your boots you can't. I haven't killed anybody, wouldn't harm a fly, you know me. Maartens is the culprit, and that nurse of his. Congenital liar, that one. She couldn't tell the truth if her life depended on it. I'm in the middle, Gene, boxed in by two people I didn't even know three months ago. Oh, well, I'll tell my story to judge and jury and Moore'll get me off. You watch . . ."

"This Maartens, you were with him when they picked you up."

"I don't deny that. We were out looking for your friend,

little Miss Philadelphia. Got tired beating the bushes, so we came into town thinking maybe she got lucky and got a ride in. Police grabbed us like a couple of hold-up men. That nurse, all sorts of wild accusations. These women are all alike, nothing but trouble. I tell you, friend, if I had known what a headache that little cousin of mine was going to be, I'd never have lifted a finger to help set things up for her father's funeral. Although he was a good sort, and you can't blame the parent for the child."

"She hasn't said anything to the police, Charles."

"She will when they catch up with her. Let me warn you, Gene, that little lady is trouble. Running around telling everybody who'll listen the most outrageous tales! Pretty embarrassing to me, I tell you! The night of the storm, that accident, she walked away in one piece, invaded the nearest house and practically turned it on its ear. I finally got her into the hospital with Maartens' help . . ."

"Did you now?"

"Not for long. She sneaked out. That's gratitude for you. Set fire to Barringer House, burned it to the ground! They catch up with her she's going to have a lot to answer for. She'll want me to stand up and witness for her, but there's little chance of that. You can only do so much, relative or no. She made her bed, she can sleep in it. I mean, how far can I go, I've my reputation to protect. She's disappeared, you know. Hiding out somewhere round here. They'll find her. I'm telling you all this not to be malicious. You know one, I'm not that sort, it's just that you were a bit smitten with her, I mean you'd be the first to admit that . . . But, believe me, she's more trouble than she's worth. I wouldn't be surprised if she and the nurse got together and deliberately cooked all this up just for spite. If I'd had any idea what a handful she was going to turn out to be, I would have taken my two weeks vacation and left town while she was up here."

"She hasn't disappeared, Charles. She's here in town."

"Here?" His voice altered in tone, apprehension seizing it.

"I found her at the Gilyard farm."

"You're mistaken. We stopped there, she wasn't there . . ."

"Yes, she was."

"No doubt she's given you some cock and bull story about Maartens and me. Well, if you want to know the truth, I hardly know the man. Anything she told you you can take with a grain of salt. As for that nurse, she and Alison ought to get together, the two of them'd make old Ananias blush with shame! Tell me what she said . . ."

"What difference does it make?"

"Doesn't make a bit of difference, that's what I'm trying to tell you! All the lying in the world can't change the facts. I haven't done anything to be ashamed of. I'll have my day in court, I'll prove it. Bet your life on that! I'm a good doctor, Gene."

"Yes, you are."

"One of the best. Got a good reputation, too. That's something you don't build up overnight. It wouldn't make much sense for me to blow up everything I've built up, would it? I'm on my way up the ladder, I am. Heading for the top! Before I'm through I'm going to be somebody!"

"I hope you are."

"You don't have to hope, it's a fact. In this world you are what you make of yourself. You should have my ambition, Gene, in two years you'd be top dog at that miserable back-water infirmary. That's all it is, all it ever will be. It doesn't make any sense at all, does it? Does it?"

"What?"

"A man, a doctor of my stature, my reputation getting involved with anything tainted with scandal . . ."

"No, it doesn't."

"Don't you believe anything you hear about me! Not one word; you're my friend, you know me better than anybody. That's the whole trouble with being successful. You're up on a pedestal and everybody wants to tear you down. Jealous, that's what they are, green with envy. She's terribly jealous of me. I knew it the first day she showed up here. Know what her trouble is? She can't accept the fact that she's a female, that her place in life is at a lower level than mine, than any man's. Spiteful creature. You look in her eyes you can see it. Filled with frustration. Be smart, get her on her train for home, nobody needs her around here, least of all you!"

"Charles . . ."

"Want to know what really happened? I'll tell you, only because you're my best friend and I know I can trust you. This Maartens, a brilliant chap, really. Top man, approached me with this idea . . ."

"Dr. Collier!"

The voice was like an axe thudding into a block of wood. They turned to the doorway. A squat, worried-looking middle-aged man stood there, briefcase in one hand, beaver in the other. "Let us not discuss our case. It's not the way we do things."

"Mr. Moore?"

"I am Franklin Moore."

Charles shot to his feet, his chains rattling. Stumbling over to the newcomer, he confronted him, seizing him by his coat, staring into his face.

"Thank God you're here! They're going to hang me, they are! You've got to stop them! You've got to tell them the truth about me! I only did what Maartens told me to do. He made me!"

"Easy easy . . ."

Around Charles' shoulder, the lawyer glanced at Gene and motioned with his head toward the door. Gene walked out, patting Charles on the shoulder as he passed. But Charles was so busy talking to Moore he never even saw him leave.

The southbound train was four minutes late arriving in Brunswick. They boarded and sat together in the last seat of the next to last car, she daubing at her eyes with the back of her sleeve, pretending it was her cold "coming out of here," he cloaked in a totally uncharacteristic dourness that all but eliminated conversation.

"It really is confusing," he said at last. "I can't imagine what he could possibly do that they might hang him for. Yet he seems convinced they're going to."

"He hasn't murdered anyone . . ."

"He's involved with a man who has. He was about to tell me the whole story when Moore walked in."

"What puzzles me is what made him tie up with a man like Maartens in the first place. Although there was one thing he said when he caught up with me in the coach, something about making more money in three days with Maartens than he could make at the hospital in a year."

"I'm afraid that's the key. He's the best friend I've ever had, he's all the good points you can think of rolled up in one personality, but like the rest of us he's got his Achilles heel. Money runs through his fingers like water. He spends and spends and spends. I lend it to him, everybody at work, down to the orderlies and the laundry help, lends to him. It sounds disloyal I know, but the fact of the matter is I haven't seen him out of debt once since the first day we met. He owes, he pays, he borrows again. The thing of it is, he just doesn't care. It's get it and spend it and if you don't have enough, borrow against what you'll get next week."

"But you can't live like that."

"It's the only way he's ever lived."

"Do you think his creditors were pressing him?"

"They're always pressing him. Not one or two, but half the town. And when Maartens came along and offered him a chance to get his hands on big money, he plunged right in."

"Maartens probably approached him knowing that his straitened circumstances would make him certain to accept any proposition that promised a lot of money."

"Damn!"

"What's the matter?"

"If that lawyer hadn't walked in when he did Charles would have told the whole story."

"It'll all come out at the trial."

"It's such a tragedy, though. Here's a man who's really an excellent doctor, established, respectable, the world his oyster. Yet he tosses it all away, reputation, future, everything for a handful of silver."

"Let's hope for his sake it won't turn out as badly as he seems to think it will."

"Alison, he was willing to let Maartens do away with you to protect their guilty secret. This is nothing small, it's got to be a capital crime."

"Well, we can talk about it all the way to Philadelphia, or we can talk about ten thousand other things."

"I'd rather talk about you. Tired?"

"A little, but still so jumpy I don't think I could sleep even if I wanted to."

The landscape swept by, the trees near naked now

against winter's impending onset, the fields drained of their green, and stripped by the wind of their wildflowers. Overhead, a flock of geese parted the sky, like a shaftless arrow shooting southward. The train sped on, the whistle sounding repeatedly warning hamlet and town of its approach, the noise and gravel flung from its wheels flushing quail from their thickets, bringing rabbits out of their warrens and squirrels out of their nests to watch the monster pass. Halfway to Portland, the countryside began thickening with farms separated by long twisting cow walls and log fences. The land continued rugged and harsh-looking, here and there great boulders heaving through as if to break free of the earth that held them fast. An occasional hill appeared crowned by woods and now and then a rill came twisting down from the distant mountains to the bottom land, the water dashing against the stones and leaping over them catching and releasing the gold of the morning sun.

They talked of many things, she of Philadelphia, of her day there, comparing life in the city to life in rural Maine.

"Do you help your mother run the house, in between teas and dinner parties?"

"I work, sir. I am a volunteer aide at the Towlton School."

"And what, pray tell, does a volunteer aide do?"

"Repair books, mostly, and keep order in class when teacher is out of the room, button shoes for little boys, wash ink off little fingers, all sorts of important chores . . ."

"Fascinating."

"I'll thank you not to scoff, Mr. Hampton. It's much more productive and meaningful than lazing around the house, sleeping till two in the afternoon, and drinking chocolate and nibbling cookies until you're ready to scream with boredom."

"And along with the school you keep busy going out with

handsome young bachelors."

"Now you're prying."

"You mentioned this Adrian fellow."

"I did? I shouldn't have. Like Barringer House, that's a part of my past I'd rather forget about."

"Tell me about him."

"You first, do you keep company with any of the nurses? Mary Elizabeth MacIntosh, for instance. She's pretty."

"Not my type, I'm afraid."

"What is your type?"

"Don't you know?"

"Perhaps we should talk about something else."

And so they began to talk of love, not directly, not explicitly, rather dwelling on likes and dislikes, the little meaningless personal things that mean so much when one you're attracted to matches each revelation with one of his own. Your favorite color. Pet hate, most glaring weakness, most embarrassing experience. Your favorite writer, artist, actor, food . . . And so they began to make astonishing discoveries about each other. He could not eat shrimp without becoming ill. She could not stomach corn without breaking out in a frightful rash, hands and face, all over . . .

He liked Byron and Keats, yellow roses and horseback riding in a gale, warm ale and sunsets. She, window shopping, Darjeeling tea, when she could get it, violets and Catawba grapes and children.

And both liked walking in the rain and ribs of beef "savagely rare." As the miles sped beneath them and they warmed to each other's presence, one by one the curtains of reserve were peeled away and friendship and love budded, flowered, and delighted the eyes of the fates that had brought them together. All thoughts of Harwich and Brunswick, of Charles and Maartens and the Gilyards, Barringer

House and storms and painful treks in the moonlight were laid by and forgotten.

And in her heart, she knew that she loved this man . . . though she scarcely knew him in one sense; in another she felt as if they had been friends a century or more. With getting to know him and letting him get to know her in turn came the intuitive knowledge, the "I knew you'd say that," "I guessed you'd like that" that usually reveals itself when two people who really care about each other communicate.

He asked a hundred questions about Philadelphia, she a hundred about Maine, about his boyhood, his parents, his brothers and sisters, his schooling, his life. For his part, he seemed fascinated by the fact that she was an only child.

"I don't think I've ever known an only child before."

"Nonsense, we're common as daisies."

"Seriously, what's it like?"

"Only is lonely, especially growing up. Brothers and sisters can talk to each other, only children must talk to dolls and pets and grown-ups."

"Pure misery. Tell me about Adrian Peale."

"We always seem to get back to him. What can I tell you? I met him at a cotillion, we started talking, he asked me to go for a Sunday carriage ride out in Merion. We stayed out to an ungodly hour . . . I never saw daddy so furious in my entire life. We liked each other, Mr. Peale and I. I guess I fell in love with him. Gene, why is it girls have such a penchant, a positive mania for tumbling head over heels for men simply because every other girl of their acquaintance is wide-eyed and squeaking over him? Honestly, if he hadn't been so la-de-dahed over, I probably wouldn't have given him a second look."

"You're asking the wrong man, I've never been la-de-dahed over."

"You would be in Philadelphia."

"Would I now? How interesting, is there a shortage of men?"

"There's no shortage of Adrian Peales."

"Is he in love with you?"

"I don't think so. I have a feeling he took me for granted, right up until the night we argued and broke up. Then, my showing a little backbone gave him second thoughts about me. He might even have begun to respect me. But, love? I doubt if he's capable of true love. Not to sound catty, it's just that when you get beneath the surface there's nothing much there. Like a striking suit of armor, lift the visor and moths fly out."

"He'd be flattered to hear that."

The train made steady progress all the way to Boston where they changed for the New York train scheduled to stop there, at Trenton and at Broad Street Station in Philadelphia. By the time they reached Philadelphia, it was well after midnight. A rainstorm arrived with them, clouds blanketing the city, slender needles driving to earth turning the streets to mud, the wheels of passing carriages picking up gobs of it and tossing them at pedestrians. Horses splashed through puddles, traffic snarled, drivers' tempers flared and the two of them ran from carriage to carriage looking for an empty one that might take them to Sedgley Avenue at the corner of Erie and the two-story brownstone house with the green shutters and the thick veil of ivy clinging to its front.

The house was in darkness and having been deprived of her key along with practically everything else save the clothes she was wearing, Alison was obliged to pound on the door.

Lydia appeared, her colorless eyes wide in astonishment, her hand holding the lamp trembling violently.

"Dear God, it's you, miss. I thought 'twas a gang of ruffians from Girard Avenue come to murder us in our beds!"

"It's raining, Lydia, may we come in?"

"Oh, my yes . . ."

They brought puddles in with them, spreading them about the foyer floor. Lydia clucked disapprovingly, but said nothing, instead hurrying into the living room and stirring the fire to life.

"How is mother?"

"Asleep."

"I know she's asleep, dear. Is she any better?"

"She's up and around. Awfully worried about you, miss. We had no idea what was happening until the telegram."

"I'm all right, a little unforeseen delay getting back, that's all. Gene, make yourself comfortable in the living room. Lydia will fix you something to eat."

"There's only a leg of mutton and cold potatoes. I suppose I could warm them. I don't go to market till Monday morning," said Lydia setting her lamp down on the table and lighting two others in turn, flooding the room with light and shadows revealing the French Provincial furniture newly purchased, according to Alison, and floor-to-ceiling velvet draperies framing the front windows.

"Pardon me for a minute, Gene, I'm going up to see mother."

"You'll not be waking her?" asked Lydia, obviously still disturbed and disoriented by their unexpected appearance. "I don't know if there's enough mutton for two. There's eggs, though. Your mother was going out tomorrow, so I didn't get much in yesterday. It's her first time out since the accident."

Alison hurried up the stairs to her mother's room. Easing the door open and taking the hall lamp with her, she entered the cloud of lavender scent that filled the room to every corner. Her mother lay in bed, her long brown braids angling away from her attractive features. She breathed easily, the covers almost imperceptibly rising and falling.

Alison went up to the bed and, sitting on the edge, bent over and kissed her on the forehead. Opening her eyes, she looked startled, blinking, reacting, and yielding to a smile as she recognized her daughter.

"Allie, Allie . . ."

They embraced, her mother patting her gently on the back, then holding her at arm's length to study her face.

"You look exhausted!"

"I'm all right."

"You'll never believe me, but I was dreaming you'd come home. What happened?"

"There was a storm the night I was to catch the train back, an accident to the coach, I was laid up for a couple of days. Nothing serious. How is your leg?"

"Good as it'll ever be. I'm up and around." She indicated the crutch lying across the chair on the opposite side of the bed. "You should see me hobbling about. Napoleon's retreat from Moscow. Did everything go all right with the funeral?"

"Yes."

"I should have been there. I'll never forgive myself. Your poor father. I miss him so. Oh, my darling, I'm so glad you're home."

"I'm sorry to wake you up out of a sound sleep."

"I should be very upset if you hadn't."

"You go back to sleep. We can talk tomorrow. I've brought a house guest home with me."

"Oh?"

"A young man, a very special young man. His name is Eugene Hampton."

"Any relation to Adelaide Hampton? You remember, her son used to be in your Sunday School class."

"I don't think so."

"Adrian Peale's been here. Camped on the doorstep. Drops by every night asking for you. Seemed very worried according to Lydia. I think he's chastened, dear. And how is cousin Charles?"

"Fine. I'll tell you all about it tomorrow."

"Such a fine young man. Your Aunt Kate, rest her soul, adored that boy. The sun rose and set on her Charles. He's certainly made a name for himself, hasn't he?"

"He certainly has. Mother, it's very late . . ."

"Yes, yes . . ." She pulled Alison to her, hugging her warmly and covering her hair with kisses. "Thank the Lord you're home at last. I thought I'd go out of my mind until the telegram came. The only comfort I had was knowing Charles was there to watch over you."

"Yes, mother. Good night."

She tucked her in, kissed her again, and went out quietly.

10

Alison slept till noon, arising feeling deliciously rested for the first time in days and so ravenously hungry she felt herself quite capable of consuming all the available legs of mutton in Philadelphia.

After breakfast she and Gene sat with Mrs. Collier in the living room and between them told the entire story. Alison had made up her mind before getting out of bed that sooner or later her mother would have to know everything. She had never made a practice of concealing the truth from either of her parents and Gene agreed that they should tell all, rather than allow Charles' perfidy to reveal itself bit by bit, as it surely would in the newspapers during the coming weeks.

"How perfectly ghastly!" exclaimed Mrs. Collier. "To think that our own flesh and blood should be mixed up in such a terrible business!"

"In all fairness, mother, we don't really know the full nature of the 'business.' "

"Alison may be called back to Maine to testify at the trial," observed Gene bluntly. "She's about the only reliable witness the state will be able to call on."

"Gracious, you mean you're turning around and traipsing right back to that awful place?"

"It's not an awful place, mother."

"It's not Philadelphia, my dear."

"I'm sure it will only be for a day or two," said Gene.

"It was only for two days last time. Seemed more like two months! Alison, you must get in touch with Dr. Logan and tell him you're back."

"Dr. Logan is headmaster at the school where I work," explained Alison. "We can stop by there, if you don't mind."

"Lead the way."

"I wouldn't bandy this dreadful business and your part in it about town if I were you, dear," said Mrs. Collier. "I can't imagine what excuse you'd make for Charles."

"I feel very sorry for him," said Alison. "I doubt very much if he ever dreamed what he was getting into."

The Towlton School was two blocks up the street from the Market Street market. The early afternoon sun was bright, streaming across the rooftops and around the cupola at the south end of the market sheds. All the sheds were closed on Sunday and the immediate area spared the cries of the fruit and vegetable hawkers and the noise of the shopping crowd. Alison met and spoke with her employer, blaming her prolonged absence on "illness while away" in lieu of the full story. This duty seen to, she and Gene began walking about town taking in the sights.

Victorian Philadelphia, like so many of its sister cities in the United States and abroad, was an amalgamation of more than a dozen towns locked together for mutual protection, progress, and anticipated prosperity. By the early 1850s the wealthier families had begun to build houses in the Italian style architecture, great square buildings of yellow stucco that stood out from groups of older brownstones like blocks of gold in peat. The Italian influence brought with it columned porticoes and surrounding gardens, past their prime so late in the year, but artistically laid out nevertheless and at each location protected from the street by spiked iron fences.

Philadelphia was a lovely city and Gene remarked on it. Large trees in abundance sentineled the cobble-stoned streets, and despite the lateness of the year songbirds still occupied their branches, filling the air with their cheerful music.

Vine and Cherry, Poplar and Pine, Walnut and Chestnut, Cypress and Buttonwood, nearly every tree in the forest named a street in the City of Brotherly Love. It was a clean city, a visibly proud city, steeped as it was in one hundred seventy years of history inaugurated by William Penn's "Holy Experiment."

By mid-afternoon, however, they tired of walking and returned by carriage to the house. Mrs. Collier had gone out and they were left in reasonable privacy by Lydia. That evening, Alison took Gene to Spauldings for dinner. The restaurant was mobbed and they had to wait nearly a half hour for a table, but they were finally given one in the center of the main dining room and their presence was noticed by a waiter some twenty minutes later. The local blue laws closed Spauldings and every other restaurant in town at eight-thirty sharp on Sundays, so having been twice delayed already, they were obliged to place their order, sit back, and hope that their meal would be prepared and served in time for them to eat it properly before the bell rang.

Both ordered steak with all the trimmings and fortunately it arrived in reasonable time and they were able to begin eating. Halfway through their meal, a familiar voice sounded through the persistent clinking of silver and glassware and the chatter of the diners surrounding.

"Alison, my dear! Is it really you?"

Adrian Peale. On his arm was a very young and very lovely red-haired girl whom Alison did not recognize but whose nose nevertheless rose in the air as Adrian initiated introductions.

Courtesy demanded a polite invitation to join them for dinner and after eyeing Alison, Gene extended it. Adrian's friend-of-the-evening's name was Priscilla Edmunds. Alison vaguely recalled the name, the girl's father being manager of a shipping company who had frequently transacted business of one sort or another with her own father at the bank.

Adrian's unexpected appearance might have upset her. He was, after all, the last man she wanted to see. Breaking with him, cutting the thread that joined their hearts, automatically pushed them off in opposite directions. Meeting Gene, in point of fact replacing Adrian with him in the niche of her affections, underscored the breach. But sight of Adrian did not make her heart beat faster, nor slow it up, for that matter. She felt no reaction whatsoever, no disappointment, no resentment, nor their opposites. As the four of them sat small-talking she actually found herself becoming more and more amused.

It was Adrian's doing. He could not keep his eyes off Gene. His reaction to Gene's presence in her company struck her as being quite like that of a small boy who comes upon another his age in possession of something or other he himself would dearly love to have. Apart from appealing to her sense of humor, it did wonders for her ego.

If Adrian Peale had changed his mind about her worthiness when she had stood up to him in his rooms and spoken her piece, he must now have an even more favorable impression of her, seeing her with another man.

"And what do you think of the big city, Hampton?" he asked.

"Big," responded Gene quietly, his tongue in his cheek.

"Will you be in town long?"

"Only until tomorrow. I've got to get back to work."

"Of course. Funny, one thinks of Maine, one doesn't know what to think about work. Not that people up there don't work, to be sure, but it's . . . so remote, so countrified one can't imagine what it offers in the way of gainful employment. One pictures the natives rushing about muskets in hand shooting game and suchlike."

"Exactly," said Gene.

Alison could have laughed out loud. It wasn't the response Adrian had expected or had wanted and the look on his face showed his disappointment.

"Alison, I stopped by your house a number of times while you were away. You had us all very worried, my dear. We fancied you might have been captured by Indians or something."

"I was, Adrian, they made me a princess and then let me come home so I could tell mother."

"Oh, I say that's funny! This girl's got quite a sense of humor, Hampton. Wait till you get to know her as I do . . ."

"I can't wait," said Gene.

"I can," said Priscilla. "I'm hungry!" As if to punctuate her dilemma, she rattled her menu and made a face.

"Priscilla, darling, can't you see . . ."

"Kindly do not darling me, Adrian Peale! I can see and I can hear, and I'm not a fool!"

"What, pray tell, are you talking about?"

Priscilla glared, sniffed, snapped her menu closed and flung it on the table.

"I have a headache, take me home!"

"I thought you were hungry?" Adrian looked at Alison and Gene questioningly, in a too-obvious appeal for support.

"I have a headache!"

Mumbling apology, he lifted Priscilla up out of her chair by one elbow, and hurried her to the semi-privacy of the nearest potted palm. What passed between the two of them in the next sixty seconds was inaudible to either Alison or Gene, but it was clear to everyone within sight of the palm that a sudden and rather violent disagreement was taking place.

The combatants left the restaurant without saying goodbye and Alison and Gene resumed eating, he commenting on what a pleasure it was to dine with a genuine Indian princess.

"Adrian Peale . . . I like him!"

"You what?" She dropped her fork in her plate and stared.

"I'm serious. How could I possibly dislike a man who hasn't the wit nor the common sense to fall in love with you? Bless the Adrian Peales of this world."

Gene took a late Monday train from Broad Street station, although his choice of departure time did not make sense to Alison. She tried to induce him to stay over the night and leave early Tuesday morning, but he preferred to sleep on the train and thus be able to get to work the next morning.

The station was filled with travelers and their friends seeing them off. Standing on the crowded platform, oblivious of the world, of voices and faces and thundering trains, he took her in his arms and kissed her lovingly.

"Miss me, my love."

"I will, you know I will."

"If, God forbid, you're not called for the trial, when shall we see each other again?"

"I don't know. School is over in June, but that's years away."

"Eons." He touched her hair beneath her bonnet with his fingertips. "I love you, Alison Collier, I hate leaving you."

"I love you, Gene Hampton. It's funny, I think I loved you a minute after I met you."

"Oh? What took you so long?"

"Conceited brute!"

"I loved you the moment I laid eyes on you."

"That's not possible, is it?"

He stilled her with his finger to her lips and kissed her again.

"Is that the kiss of a man who exaggerates?"

A bell clanged, steam snarled at their ankles and doors began closing with the finality of guns going off up and down the line.

"You have to go," she said quietly, staring into his eyes.

"I know."

"It's leaving."

"I know."

"Gene . . ."

He sighed, released her and turned about just as the train began moving. Running alongside it, he rapped on a door and a passenger standing on the other side opened it and let him on. He turned, blew a kiss and waved. In less than a minute the train was out of the station, a black dot shrinking in size far down the track. She turned away and was suddenly filled with abject loneliness, so powerful, so all-pervasive that she unconsciously placed both hands under her heart.

Two weeks dragged by. Two weeks of letter writing, letter reading, full days at the school and lonely nights in her room in the house on Sedgley Avenue, then on the morning of the first day of November the letter she wanted strangely enough even more than his letters appeared:

Office of the County Clerk
Cumberland County, Maine

Dear Miss Collier,

You are hereby formally requested to appear as a witness for the prosecution in the pending legal action State versus Dr. Hendrik Maartens, et al, trial begin on the 10th of November instant.

Arrangements have been made for you to stay overnight at the Potters Inn in Brunswick.

Enclosed is a cheque in the sum of $75 for your trainfare and other expenses. We would be pleased if you would keep a list of all expenses incurred by you relevant this matter and if, when your duties are completed, the amount comes to a figure in excess of monies advanced you will be properly reimbursed.

Please be advised that if you fail to appear as requested, a subpoena may be issued to insure your presence at the designated time and place of trial.

If you are unable to appear due to illness or infirmity, a notarized letter of explanation from your physician must be received by this office at least one day prior to trial opening.

C. T. Hanson
County Clerk

She left on Tuesday, the ninth, on the seven o'clock train for New York, from there to Boston, Portland and Brunswick, arriving shortly after eight in the evening and being met at the station by Gene. He held her long and kissed her affectionately before either of them bothered to pick the conversation up beyond initial greetings.

News of the trial, extravagantly termed by the newspapers "The Grave Cheaters Trial," had spread all over New

England and Brunswick was swarming with the curious from all four points of the compass. Despite everyone's seeming eagerness to watch the proceedings in person, room for the public was, according to Gene, restricted, most of the available seats being delegated to newspaper reporters, some of whom had come all the way from as far south as Atlanta and as far west as Columbus, Ohio.

They sat in the musty, cigar-smoke-veiled lobby of the Potters Inn until late in the evening talking.

"I wrote you I've seen Charles again," he said.

"How does he look?"

"Not good. Black circles under his eyes, nerves in knots, spouting all sorts of nonsense, contradicting himself over and over again. As if it were all a nightmare he can't recall the plot of."

"What does he say?"

"First Maartens is to blame for everything, then Maartens is as innocent as a baby and the nurse is the mastermind."

"It was Maartens, that I'm sure of."

"That's not important, Alison. What worries me is how deeply Charles is involved. The way he's behaving he's more afraid of being hanged now than he was before you left, if that's possible."

"Have you talked to his lawyer?"

"Yesterday. He wouldn't tell me anything, naturally, I mean about the facts in the case, if he actually knows the facts. That wasn't what I wanted to find out, anyway. I was much more interested in his opinion of Charles' mental state. He told me that there are times when he's perfectly rational and under control and others when he behaves like a wild animal."

"Is he still in chains?"

"I'm afraid so, although he seems to have gotten used to

them. I hate to say it, darling, but his mind may be becoming affected, if it's not already."

"I know, I've thought about that myself. What can we do?"

"There doesn't seem to be anything anyone can do. Luckily, Moore is a good lawyer and seems to feel genuine sympathy for Charles."

"What he needs is a doctor. Couldn't one of the doctors from the hospital talk to him?"

"Charles wouldn't like that, not in his present frame of mind. He practically threw me out on my ear. He looks you in the eye, goes along talking calmly, rationally, then all of a sudden bang goes his temper."

"Poor man. Will all of them be tried at the same time?"

"Starting out they will."

"Even Alma and Otto? Otto . . ." She paused and shook her head. "He's more like a puppy than a man, despite his size and his face. He and Alma aren't really a part of this, Gene."

"They'll neither of them be tried. It'll be Maartens, Charles, the nurse and Mueller."

"Mueller? Where have I heard that name before?"

"He's the funeral director in Harwich. Charles sent your father's casket over to him for his people to bring on to the cemetery."

"Miss Collier?"

They looked up. A young, pasty-faced man with thick spectacles lifted his hat in greeting.

"Yes?"

"Permit me to introduce myself. I'm Joshua Frame, assistant to Mr. Boggs, the County Attorney. Mr. Boggs has asked me to arrange for your written deposition."

"Written? I thought I was going to have to testify on the witness stand."

"You probably will, but we'd like to have your sworn statement for his honor, Mr. Justice Whitfield, before the trial opens. Would it be all right for you to come to the courthouse about an hour before, at say nine o'clock? Room D on the second floor."

"I'll be there."

"Nine o'clock. Thank you." The ghostly stranger reset his hat on his head and drifted off across the lobby, still crowded from door to desk with out-of-towners.

"It's just your story in writing," said Gene.

"I'll do it before I go to sleep. Oh Gene, darling, I knew it would come to this."

"To what?"

"I'd have to roll up my sleeves and pitch in and help them build their case against him. I know it's the law, I know it's right, but it seems so downright disloyal."

"I know, but I'm afraid you'll have to do it. I'll probably be called myself. It's a sorry world when you're asked to turn against your friend when he needs you most."

"I wish you wouldn't put it that way, it's so damnably true."

She glanced at her watch.

"What time is it?" he asked.

"After ten."

"You'd better go up, darling. You'll need your rest for tomorrow."

"I just adore the idea of getting up in front of the whole world and telling what I know. Do you suppose they'll arrest me for burning the house down?"

"Somehow I doubt it," he said smiling.

Walking her to the front desk, he got her room key for her, gave it to her at the foot of the stairs, kissed her good night and left.

11

She handed in her deposition at nine o'clock and lingered about the front of the courthouse waiting for Gene to appear and watching the crowd gather. Mr. Butters, although somewhat perturbed over Gene's absence from the hospital on Monday, had little choice but to grant him the time off requested by the defense. He had volunteered to act as a character witness for Charles.

They took their seats at nine-thirty, as luck would have it two rows behind Franklin Moore at the defense table. Promptly at ten the clerk ordered the crammed courtroom to rise, loudly announced Mr. Justice Whitfield, and in strutted a gnarled little gamecock, robes flying after him like sails wind-ripped from the mast, a ponderous black book under one arm and with his free hand seemingly pulling himself forward by his beard in his haste to mount his throne of authority.

Mr. Justice Whitfield was in reality Judge Whitfield, but word had gotten around that he much preferred the former title. And evidently the world deferred to his wishes. Evident as well was his deep and abiding affection for his beard. It was a barometer as to his state of mind. Tugging it indicated serious doubt, gently caressing it, preening it agreement, and scratching it, according to Gene:

"Confusion *and* an itch."

"Ssssh . . ."

Alison glanced about the courtroom as they waited for the prisoners to be marched in and seated on the empty bench along the wall to the judge's left. The place had been newly painted for the occasion, a sepulchral gray with white trim. Mr. Justice Whitfield's small head supported by his beard and held aloft with a dignity that bordered on the absurd was haloed by a round-topped window in the center of the rear wall. Through the windows on the left under the upstairs hallway down which she had walked earlier to deliver her written version of the events at Barringer House and elsewhere, a cold November sun sent shafts of white light across the gathering.

She recognized a familiar-looking couple seated behind the County Attorney and his battery of assistants, Mr. and Mrs. Gately, parents of the girl restored to life by Dr. Maartens on that unforgettable night in Barringer House.

A door opened and two uniformed guards led the shackled male prisoners into the courtroom, seating them on the bench. Following them, Nurse Raphael appeared, free of irons and sitting as far away from Maartens on her left as the length of the bench allowed.

The trial began, the County Attorney unfolding the case against the prisoners, pausing occasionally for whispered assistance from one or another of his juniors. Boggs struck Alison as somewhat arrogant, very sure of his ground and palpably determined to convict the accused and see them punished to the full extent of the law. With Mr. Justice Whitfield's permission, he called his first witness. Mr. Gately took the chair.

"Your name, sir?"

"Owen Acton Gately."

"Your business, Mr. Gately?"

"I am a dealer in lumber and hides."

"Mr. Gately, you have a daughter, is that correct?"

"Yes, sir, Miriam."

"How old is Miriam?"

"Twenty her last birthday."

"Is your daughter in good health at the present time?"

"At the present time, yes."

"Is she generally healthy?"

"Pretty much so."

"Has she been ill lately?"

"Last October second she woke up in the morning vomiting blood. In my opinion, she had . . ."

"Objection, your honor!" Franklin Moore was on his feet, along with Maartens' attorney who was also, Alison gathered, representing Nurse Raphael. "The witness is not a qualified doctor of medicine and his opinion . . ."

"Sustained," said Mr. Justice Whitfield, smoothing his beard. Boggs continued:

"When you discovered your daughter in this condition, did you call a doctor?"

"No. We had only been living here for two months and we didn't know any doctors, so I took her straight to the hospital in Harwich, the East Cumberland County Hospital."

"At the hospital was a doctor assigned to examine Miriam?"

"Yes, sir."

"Is that doctor in this courtroom now? If so, would you point to him?"

Alison's eyes went to Charles sitting on the bench, his head bowed, eyes studying the floor, paying no attention to Gately's identifying finger.

"Dr. Charles Collier."

"Yes, sir, he's the one."

"Your honor, with your permission may the record show that the witness has identified Dr. Charles Collier."

"Done."

"Mr. Gately, did you stay at the hospital and wait while your daughter was being examined by Dr. Collier?" asked Boggs.

"Yes, sir."

"And when the doctor was finished, did he speak with you?"

"He did. He told me in his opinion Miriam had an ulcer and that she would need bedrest and care and a very strict diet. He told me it would be best if she remained at the hospital for a few days."

"Was that all that you and he discussed?"

"Sir?"

"Did he, for example, talk about her health otherwise, how strong or how weak she was, her heart . . ."

"Objection, your honor!" Again Moore was on his feet and waving his hand. "Counsel is leading the witness."

Mr. Justice Whitfield leaned over and studied Gately. "I see no ring in this man's nose. Overruled!" The gavel pounded, the crowd laughed, the loudest laughter of all coming from Mr. Justice Whitfield.

"Did your daughter have a weak heart, sir?"

"I really can't say. No doctor ever told us she did, but she wasn't exactly robust."

"How long was she in the hospital?"

"She remained there all that day and all the next day. Her mother and I went to visit her both days."

"And did she seem improved?"

"She seemed cheerful."

"What did Dr. Collier say?"

"He told us that he was a little concerned about the

hemorrhaging, but that he was keeping a close watch on it."

"Then what happened?"

"Late the second night, actually about three in the morning the hospital sent a man over to our house with word that Miriam had died suddenly in her sleep. My wife fainted at the news. I myself was so shocked I could hardly stand."

"What did you do then?"

"I put my wife back in bed and called a neighbor, Mrs. Grafton, to sit with her. And I went over to the hospital."

"Did you see Dr. Collier?"

"Yes, he took me in to see Miriam's body. He told me she'd had a heart attack. He'd already filled out the death certificate. He was very sympathetic."

"He told you the reason for her death was a heart attack? And you say you saw her body?"

"Yes, in the hospital morgue. It was terrible, her lips, her skin . . . awful!"

"What did you do then?"

"Dr. Collier gave me a glass of brandy and sat and talked with me. He seemed very upset by what had happened, but he claimed that such things do occur, although rarely, and that there was nothing that he could have done to save her. It just happened too fast. He suggested Miriam's body be removed to a funeral home right away to prepare it for burial."

"And did he suggest which funeral home?"

"Mueller's in Harwich."

"What then?"

"He offered to make the necessary arrangements. I was in no state to do anything, so I told him to go ahead."

"Did you go to Mueller's the next day?"

"Yes, I couldn't sleep the rest of the night and I was exhausted, but my nerves had settled down somewhat. The brandy helped and the doctor gave me some medicine."

"You met Mr. Mueller?"

"Yes, sir."

"Is Mr. Mueller in this courtroom?"

Gately pointed to Mueller.

"Him."

"Your honor, may the record show that the witness has identified Herman Walter Mueller. Now, Mr. Gately, I'm going to ask you an important question and I would like you to take the time to think it over carefully before you answer. Mr. Gately, when you were at the funeral home did you have occasion to converse with Mr. Mueller on any matters other than the funeral arrangements?"

"Yes, sir."

"What did you talk about?"

"Mr. Mueller was very sympathetic. I remember he kept saying over and over again what a tragedy it was for such a young girl to die. With her whole life ahead of her, and all that. He had tears in his eyes. Then, I don't know how it happened, but we got around to talking about Dr. Maartens."

"Dr. Hendrik Maartens?"

"Yes, the prisoner there."

"What did Mr. Mueller tell you about Dr. Maartens?"

"He said that he had heard some very strange and marvelous things about him."

"What marvelous things?"

"Specifically that he had taken a young boy who had been pronounced dead and brought him back to life, somehow, some way started his heart beating again. Mueller claimed the boy actually came back to life. And was now still living and perfectly healthy."

"What was your reaction to this?"

"I don't recall my having much of any reaction. I was still pretty upset. But then Mueller said something that started me thinking. He told me the only reason he'd brought such a thing up was that Miriam's case was so similar to the boy's."

"Did he identify this boy by name?"

"No, but he did say that this resurrection, reincarnation, whatever you call it, took place over in Albany, New York, just last year and also that Dr. Maartens was presently living at Barringer House."

"Did you inquire of Mueller whether or not he knew Maartens personally?"

"No, even though I thought about it, I didn't put much stock in it, not right away at any rate."

"But you eventually changed your mind?"

"Yes, I got home about noontime and got to talking about it with my wife. I don't know how we got around to it, but I mentioned what Mueller had said about Dr. Maartens and the boy in Albany. Althea, Mrs. Gately, seized on it. She insisted I get in touch with Maartens right away."

"Did you?"

"Not that day. I wanted to think about it. But Althea kept at me and early in the evening I went back to see Mueller. Anyway, he arranged for me to meet with Maartens the following morning. Oddly enough, the more I thought about it, the less preposterous it seemed. I guess it was because we had everything to gain and nothing to lose."

"You met Maartens?"

"At Barringer House, yes. He was very solicitous, very kind; he told me all about the boy, answered all my questions. I told him about Miriam. I asked him outright if he thought he could do anything. At first he seemed hesitant about getting involved."

"Did he offer any reasons for delaying a decision?"

"He told me that it was a technique that was still in its infancy and that there was no guaranteeing the results, in spite of his success in Albany. Also that because of the nature of the thing, absolute secrecy was a must. It would mean that if he agreed to try with Miriam, Mrs. Gately and I must be sworn to silence. We'd even have to sign a paper swearing that we had never even met Maartens."

"You were willing to do this?"

"Why not? Wouldn't you? Wouldn't anybody?"

The gavel sounded. "The witness will confine himself to answers only," said Mr. Justice Whitfield.

"In this first meeting with Maartens, did the doctor mention money?"

"He didn't, I did. I told him straight out that I'd give him every penny I had if he could do it. If he was successful."

"And what was his reaction?"

"He said not to worry about money. The important thing was time. If there was any chance in the world of bringing Miriam back to life, he would have to go to work at once. Althea and I asked his permission to discuss it with Dr. Collier, figuring he might be able to help, but Maartens adamantly refused. He kept stressing the necessity for secrecy, insisting that letting the word out could wreck everything. That made sense to us."

"Of course. What did you do next?"

"I signed an agreement to pay him twenty-five thousand dollars if he were successful and another ten thousand if Miriam was still alive six months later. Oh, my God . . ."

The clerk handed Boggs a glass of water and he in turn handed it to Gately who sipped a little, regained his composure and went on. "Then I told Mueller that Maartens was taking over."

"At this point your daughter had not yet been buried . . ."

"Oh, yes, the funeral was held the afternoon of the day she died."

"You and your wife attended, of course."

"Yes."

"You saw your daughter in her casket?"

"No, it was closed, but there was no mistaking the casket. It was hers, all right. I know, I picked it out. I saw her for the last time that morning at the funeral home, then at Barringer House that awful night . . ."

Gately proceeded to tell about the ceremony, the first night's abortive attempt to restore life to Miriam, how it was called off by Maartens when the old woman collapsed and how the next night Miriam was brought back to life.

"And where is your daughter now?"

"Visiting relatives in New Hampshire. That was part of the agreement, that she should go away. It's obvious why . . . now."

"Is she healthy?"

"Perfectly."

"And would you please tell the court, what exactly prompted you to appear in this courtroom today?"

Gately pointed at Nurse Raphael. "It was all over town, the story she told. That the whole thing was a hoax, a cruel sham, a device for extorting money from grieving parents and relatives."

"Objection, your honor!" exclaimed Franklin Moore, "the witness is citing hearsay."

"Sustained," said the judge, "the witness must confine his statements to what he himself knows in this matter."

Two other witnesses for the prosecution, neither familiar to Alison, were called to the stand in turn by Boggs after Mr. Gately. Both men had had members of their immediate families similarly "restored to life" by Dr. Maartens and his associates. It became apparent that the fee for this unique service varied according to what the traffic would bear. Gately had paid twenty-five thousand dollars with a promise of additional monies. In another case, a man and wife had handed over the deed to six hundred forty prime acres of farmland in return for the revival of their only son. In the third case, an eighty-foot sloop constituted payment for bringing a sea captain's young wife back to him.

It took virtually the entire day for all three witnesses to tell their stories to the court and undergo cross-examination at the hands of Franklin Moore and the other defense attorney. Like Gately, the other witnesses had been prompted by Nurse Raphael's confession to come forward.

On the morning of the second day, the trial began with Dr. Maartens on the stand.

"Your name?"

"Dr. Hendrik Maartens."

"Hendrik Maartens, Louis Hoorn, Theo Vanderweg and what other names?" asked Boggs.

"I am a doctor of medicine; you will address me properly. Your honor, I protest!" Maartens was on his feet, his pale face reddening. Gene leaned toward Alison.

"This is going to take two days."

The business of Maartens' title straightened out to his satisfaction, the questioning resumed. Alison listened, but could not take her eyes off Charles, who sat like a dead man upright, staring blankly into space, his mind miles away.

According to Maartens' testimony, he had come to North America in 1842, ten years earlier, from Leyden in Holland where he explained conceitedly that he had conducted a thriving practice, and feeling a warm affinity for the community at large had charitably given of his limited free time to instructing classes in pathology at the local medical school. Leaving Holland, he settled in Montreal, living there and practicing for seven years. In Montreal he had met Nurse Raphael. Twice he was silenced by Mr. Justice Whitfield, however, for calling her down for her "lies" and "distortions."

The questioning then turned to his association with Dr. John Devereaux. At this point, Maartens suddenly refused to go on. His attorney waived cross-examination and he was temporarily excused with the judge's admonition that "he was not to think for a moment that he had any right under the law to refrain from responding to questions put to him by learned counsel, that he was only being excused for the time being so as not to delay matters."

"I will give you to dwell upon the error of your ways. If you persist in refusing to answer future questions, I will hold you in contempt of this court and it will go hard with you."

Nurse Raphael was next to testify and as expected she proved more than willing to tell everything she knew. Maartens interrupted her repeatedly, until finally the judge's patience deserted him and he ordered the bailiff to remove the doctor from the courtroom. The story she related was so shocking, so bizarre and yet so incredible in the extent of the audacity of the participants that her audience gasped and oohed and ahhed repeatedly. For her part, Alison was not surprised at what she heard, not in the face of Gately's testimony and her own experience. It was all so simple and so logical when the strings were untied, the wrappings removed and the works revealed. Credit for the scheme in the nurse's view went to Dr. Maartens, although to the best of Alison's own recollection it was Devereaux who claimed authorship.

Nurse Raphael finished her story, her voice rising to a near scream as she continued flinging accusations about like stones. Cross-examined by the defense, she stuck to her testimony and was subsequently excused.

Alison's heart began pounding as Charles was identified, sworn and seated. His eyes had a glazed look and even though he seemed to be staring directly at her he failed to see her. The questioning proceeded and he answered promptly, although now and again his voice would descend to a whisper, compelling Mr. Justice Whitfield to urge him to speak up.

"Doctor," said Boggs grimly, "you are under oath. With that in mind, would you tell this court truthfully whether or not Miriam Gately was actually dead when you sent the orderly to so inform her parents."

"She was alive."

"Speak up, please, I can't hear you."

"She was alive!"

"Did you or did you not administer a drug in secrecy which lent her the appearance of death?"

"I did. I put her into coma."

"She was barely breathing, isn't that so? Her lips, her flesh . . ."

"She looked dead."

"Isn't it a fact that you had previously made a bargain with Dr. Maartens naming a price of six thousand dollars in exchange for which you would fake Miriam Gately's death?"

"He made the price, I didn't."

"Nevertheless, you agreed to that figure."

"Yes."

"You received the same amount for simulating death in the other two cases as well, informing the witnesses of the deaths of their loved ones and recommending that the 'bodies' be removed to Mueller's Funeral Home."

"Yes."

"In the case of Miriam Gately, how long did you plan to keep her in this state of suspended animation, as it were?"

"As long as necessary, a week or more if we had to."

"If you had to. What would you have done if she woke up at the funeral home?"

"There was no chance of that. The drug was measured exactly. Mueller kept close watch on her and if she had given any sign of reviving prematurely, all he'd have to do would be to administer an additional dosage."

"So now we have fraud cloaked in the dignified robes of science. Doctor, are we to understand that you agree essentially with Nurse Raphael's testimony, which you have heard, that when the patient, in this case Miriam Gately, was revived during the so-called ceremony at Barringer House it was merely the wearing off of the drug, abetted by a saucer of common spirits of ammonia?"

"Yes."

"Yes. The entire scheme, therefore, was a hoax purposefully, nay deliberately designed and executed to extract money from the relatives of these unfortunate individuals. Absolute bunkum!"

"Yes."

"It was Dr. Maartens' idea?"

"So I understand."

"How did you first meet Dr. Maartens?"

"Through Herman."

"Mr. Mueller. You were, according to Nurse Raphael's testimony, in dire straits financially. Is that correct?"

"I was in debt up to my ears."

"And you saw this despicable machination then as an opportunity to realize a large sum of money for very little effort, correct?"

"Yes."

"Albeit no small amount of danger to Miriam Gately and the other two young people."

"There was no danger. There was never any danger. They were young, strong, I examined them thoroughly. I never would have gone ahead if there'd been any danger!"

"You say they were all three young. I assume that you select these people with great care. What were the criteria for selection?"

"They had to be ill, with something that carried with it the possibility, no matter how slim, of dying. And they couldn't die in surgery."

"Why not?"

"It would have involved other staff members unnecessarily. I got them in and out very fast. The office took my word for it that they had died. I signed all three death certificates. I myself removed the bodies to the morgue."

"Correction, doctor, not 'bodies,' but living people."

"Yes."

"Continue."

"They had to be young, with most of their lives still before them. Dr. Maartens said that nobody would pay to bring a seventy-year-old back to life, and he was right. Oh, somebody might, but the odds came down considerably when we dealt with younger people."

"That makes sense, if any sense can be made of this monstrous nightmare. Let us go back to the beginning. What was your reaction when Dr. Maartens first approached you with the idea? Were you repelled by it?"

"Yes, also attracted by it, fascinated."

"With the idea or with the prospect of all that money?"

"I needed the money desperately. You can't begin to know how desperately . . ."

"I don't think any of us wants to know. More important, were you aware at the time that Maartens had already perpetrated this abominable hoax not once, but three times in Albany?"

"So he told me. We talked a long time before the first one. We disagreed on a number of things."

"Using the old woman. I was against that. But he insisted she lent a sort of carnival atmosphere that the people we were duping rather expected."

"In other words he believed it necessary to put on a show for them."

"I guess so."

"Tell me, doctor, all three attempts were successful, but what would you have done if the results had been different?"

"The results couldn't have been different. I told you, I examined all three patients myself personally."

"I'm not talking about the patients, I'm talking about their relatives. You heard Mr. Gately testify yesterday that Mrs. Gately fainted dead away at the news. What if she had had a weak heart, what if instead of fainting, the shock of hearing of Miriam's death had induced a fatal heart attack?"

"It didn't."

"No thanks to you and your friends! How long did you and Maartens intend continuing this unconscionable deception?"

"We planned on four attempts. That was to be the limit. If anybody at the hospital had ever found out that any of the four people had been brought back to life they might have put two and two together."

"Inasmuch as you were the attending physician in all the

cases, were you ever concerned over the possibility of one or another of the relatives letting the word slip?"

"No, never. They were extremely grateful. Any one of them was practically ready to cut off his right arm for Maartens after what he'd done for them."

"Nevertheless, you and he were both afraid that one way or another the cat might get out of the bag."

"Yes, that's what happened in Albany. That's why he had to move on."

"And the revived 'corpse' was always sent away immediately after being brought back to life. To New Hampshire or the Canary Islands or wherever."

"No one could know they'd been brought back to life. Where they were sent nobody knew that they'd 'died.' The excuse we gave the relatives was that if it got out, it would have turned the world upside down."

"No question about that. And sending them packing was a small price for the 'miracle' you five wrought, although in addition to the rather big price everybody seemed willing to pay!"

Boggs finished questioning Charles and was unable to resist following up with a short speech having to do with ethics and morals and the need for every patient's absolute trust in his physician, adding caustically that accused's outrageous violation of that trust was, in his view, "as heinous a crime as cold-blooded murder!" Charles took it all without comment, lapsing back into his previous state of glazed eyes and semi-awareness.

Alison, Gene and Mr. Butters were called by the defense as character witnesses for Charles and the day ended on a fruitful note for the newsgatherers assembled in the courtroom and outside in the street, reams of sensational copy tumbling into their laps.

Gene rented a gig for a ride in the country that evening, for the announced purpose of shedding, if only temporarily, their consciousness of the day's events.

It was a lovely evening, bright and clear, with a playful breeze that lacked the marrow-seeking chill consistently characterizing the November winds of the region. Despite the welcome break in the cold weather and the chance to get out of Brunswick for an hour or so, neither of them was in a particularly happy frame of mind. Franklin Moore had inadvertently let slip that despite their testimony in Charles' behalf and his own willingness to cooperate with the prosecution he still faced life imprisonment, if not the hangman's noose.

Wheeling along the narrow road, the moon casting its glow down upon the horse's flank, they passed by the cemetery. The iron gates were closed and locked for the night. Up to that time on the long ride from Brunswick, neither had mentioned the trial, but sight of the cemetery recalled the grisly tableau of Otto and Dr. Devereaux removing the casket from the grave at the top of the hill on the evening of the storm.

"It had to be Miriam Gately's empty casket," remarked Gene. "Remember what Mr. Gately said?"

"That she'd been buried that afternoon, before he'd decided to go ahead with Maartens?"

"That's right. She never was buried, of course, but her casket was and Maartens and the others knew that her father could identify it. So they made sure they had it at Barringer House when both Gatelys showed up for the ceremony. Just one more prop."

"I've been wondering about something else," said Alison, "this business of perpetrating the hoax four times only and then moving on."

"You know all the reasons for that."

"But why would Charles agree to such an arrangement? Maartens and the others planned to move on after the fourth one, but what was Charles supposed to do? Particularly after Miriam and the others came back after their 'vacations'? He stays behind and runs the risk of word getting out and who knows what happening . . ."

"I don't think he gave that much thought," said Gene. "He had one thing in mind, get his hands on the money. I doubt if he could see clearly past that, could see or wanted to."

"He got nearly twenty thousand dollars. I wonder how much is left?"

"No more than a couple thousand, I'm sure, and that'll have to be returned."

"How is he going to pay his attorney?"

"He won't, but don't worry about Moore. He's getting more newspaper copy out of this business than he ever dreamed. He'll be able to pick his spots and name his price for the rest of his life."

They were heading back toward Brunswick now, the horse loping along briskly. On the right, just before the familiar stand of pine trees the Gilyard farm appeared. Alison would have liked to stop by to say hello, but no lights showed and rather than awaken the couple, she suggested that they come out the following day after the day's session concluded.

It was after nine by the time they returned to the Potters Inn. No sooner had they walked into the crowded lobby than they were approached by a middle-aged man with dark curly hair and a younger companion, both wearing badges on their vests and exuding the confidence of authority.

"Detective Paley and this is Detective Thomas Burkett.

May we have a word with you, miss?" asked the older man.

She nodded, introduced Gene, and the four of them found chairs around a floorstand ashtray piled with cigar stubs, prompting Burkett to request Alison's permission to light up. She smiled and nodded and he put a match to a monstrous black cigar.

Thomas Burkett, she thought . . . but not detective, sergeant. Of course! The clipping from the Albany newspaper, the three inches of print on pulp that had sent John Devereaux to his death. Thomas Burkett had come up in the world. But it was Paley, the older of the two, who did most of the talking:

"Miss Collier, we come'd over from Albany to take Dr. Maartens back with us. The papers has been signed and the County Attorney's agreed to let us take him back to stand trial for murdering a lady name of Eleanor Lyons."

"That means they're finished with him here," said Gene, glancing at Alison. "And they hardly even started. What a shame."

"The Lyons case takes precedence," said Burkett.

"I'm sure, it's just that we were hoping that when Maartens testifies tomorrow he might say something to make things a little easier for Dr. Collier. Although God knows if anything can help at this point," said Gene.

"Mr. Boggs is questioning Maartens in private right now," said Paley, "and he'll be getting a written paper. When it's handed over to the judge he'll probably read it in open court. It might have something in it to help the other fellow."

"It might make things even worse for him," said Alison ruefully.

"You don't think Collier is guilty?" asked Burkett, mystified.

"I'd rather not get into that," she said.

Paley took out a yellow envelope. "This is for you, miss. The reward."

"Reward for what?"

"They's been a standing offer of one thousand dollars for information leading to the arrest of Louis Hoorn . . . Maartens. His honor, Mayor Dawkins of Albany has decided that you is entitled to it."

"I don't see how, it was Nurse Raphael who got them all arrested."

"May be, but we ain't in the habit of giving rewards to guilty parties," continued Paley. "The way the mayor put it you is the plucky girl what got away from that bunch and that was what really led to their downfall, if you follow my meaning . . . Hoorn'd never have been arrested if he'd been able to keep you locked up. He would have been home and able to handle the nurse instead of running about the countryside. Mayor Dawkins' orders, miss," he added, tendering the envelope.

She accepted it and both officers got to their feet, putting their hats on.

"Been a pleasure meeting you, folks," said Burkett.

"Likewise," said Paley. "Oh, I most forgot." He took out a stub of pencil and a crumpled piece of paper. "Got to ask you to sign for the money, if you don't mind."

She did as he requested, although not particularly relishing the idea of being rewarded for indirectly helping to send Charles away for what might be the rest of his life. When the two policemen had disappeared out the door, she revealed her feelings to Gene.

"Alison, I love you," he said smiling, "and when one loves another you take the little faults with the big good points."

"Precisely what little fault are you referring to, Mr. Hampton?"

"My darling, you do have the most annoying habit of curry combing ethics till they glow. You worry about burning Barringer House down when you only started the fire to save your life. You worry about getting up in court and telling the truth for fear of hurting him and now you feel strangely about accepting a reward for helping catch Maartens, even when you know in your heart that if you hadn't done what you did he'd still be running loose."

"I just don't want it." Opening the envelope, she took out a cashier's draft for a thousand dollars drawn on the National Bank of Albany. "It's like blood money!"

"Take my advice, darling. Put it in the bank and forget about it. When this whole dismal carnival is packed up and moved on into memory, you'll feel differently. Take it over to Henry Porier at the Brunswick Citizens first thing tomorrow morning. Henry is a good friend of mine, tell him you know me and he'll take special care of you and your fortune. Speaking of tomorrow, I won't be at the trial."

"Why not?"

"They're through with me. I character witnessed for Charles and that's it."

"So did I, so they won't need me, either."

"No, I think they'll probably call you once more, to go over your story. That's the real reason they fetched you back up here in the first place. When you're done, get Moore or one of Boggs' assistants to run you over to the hospital. I'll try to get off work soon as you get there."

"You know what this means, I'll be heading home tomorrow."

"What's wrong with that?"

"Alone. When will you come down to Philadelphia again?"

"That's hard to say. As soon as I possibly can."

"Please, make it sooner than that."

She was up and out and at the bank waiting for it to open at nine in the morning. Henry Porier requested her endorsement, took her check, asked to be remembered to Gene, asked how the trial was going and bid her good day.

The third day of the trial of Drs. Maartens and Collier, Nurse Raphael and Herman Walter Mueller, without Maartens, began at ten-fifteen, Mr. Justice Whitfield having, in his words, "been delayed by the loss of a wheel from my carriage coming over from my hotel."

It was a gloomy, winter's-coming day that succeeded early in penetrating Alison's soul and rooting a mood of melancholy.

Mueller was questioned by the prosecution and by the defense, returned clankingly to his place on the prisoners' bench, and Alison was called.

No sooner had she taken the witness chair, the bailiff announcing that she had already been sworn, than Boggs fixed her with a look that told her she was the one he was waiting for. Intuitively, she knew that he wanted her to verbally crucify Charles, on the heels as it were of her previous day's testimony to his character. Should Boggs succeed, it would be the brightest star in his crown. To have a blood relative of the accused disavow that consanguineous bond in favor of agreement with the accusations of his guilt was a prize well worth going after.

But she was not about to oblige him. She told herself that she would answer truthfully, but she would not be led into any traps that would make it any worse than it was already for Charles.

Boggs began by going over old ground, covering her written deposition. But when he arrived at the circumstances surrounding her second attempt at escape and Charles' catching up with her in the coach and bringing her back to the house, he began probing into her reaction to Charles' conduct, in particular his unwillingness to interfere with Maartens' plans to do away with her. She hesitated in answering some of his questions, and twice inquired of Mr. Justice Whitfield if she had to answer.

Boggs hurried his questions in an effort to push her into a corner, urging her to agree that Charles was as much a murderer in his heart as Maartens was in actuality.

"Objection, your honor," exclaimed Franklin Moore, shooting to his feet. "Learned counsel is badgering his own witness!"

"This witness is hostile, your honor!" snapped Boggs.

"He is endeavoring to put words in her mouth!" exclaimed Moore.

"Both of you gentlemen kindly approach the bench," said the judge, tugging at his beard. They did so, whispering briefly among them, then Moore sat down and Boggs returned to his examination of the witness.

"I will withdraw the last question. Let me ask you this, Miss Collier. In your written statement given this court did you or did you not state that just prior to the prisoner's ordering the driver to turn the coach around and go back to Barringer House you told him to his face that he had willingly and unhesitatingly deferred to the will of a madman? Your very words, Miss Collier. Your own cousin was willing to see you die rather than risk his own skin! You know he said that, you know what your response was when he said it. Here is a man, a pitiful excuse for a human being is what you called him, Miss Collier. Again, your own words, here is a pitiful excuse for a human being who deliberately brought you back to Barringer House from where you had escaped earlier with great difficulty and hardship. Drugged you, brought you back, turned you over to Maartens and agreed without blinking an eye to his suggestion that you be murdered to insure your silence. Brought you back to the house a second time, tried to catch you when you subsequently got away, would have killed you himself . . ."

"Objection!"

"Objection sustained, that is a conclusion, Mr. Boggs, with no basis in fact."

"Very well, your honor," said Boggs, a trace of irritation in his voice. "Miss Collier, let me put it this way. Can you deny in your heart that your cousin, Dr. Charles Collier, is a callous, unprincipled, thoroughly despicable . . ."

"Yes, I deny it!"

Boggs leered and tossed his hands high.

"Ah, I'm beginning to understand. Your honor, gentlemen of the jury, it's all becoming abundantly clear, the sun is out flooding the mind . . ."

Mr. Justice Whitfield rapped his gavel. "May we curtail the rhetoric, sir, and get to the point?"

"Your honor, this man Charles Collier is not one man, but two. On the one hand, a monster capable of the most heinous criminal conduct, on the other a kind-hearted, charitable soul, thoughtful and considerate . . . Is that what you would have this court believe, Miss Collier?"

"Yes!"

Boggs' jaw dropped and his eyes started from his head. "You . . ."

"I believe that Charles Collier did not know what he was doing the night he brought me back to Barringer House and after that. I believe it quite possible that his mind had become affected."

"You're not serious!"

"I am. He may not have even known what he was doing, at least a good part of the time."

"Your honor," said Boggs, "the witness is wandering far afield. She is no alienist, how can she possibly know what was in the defendant's mind?"

"You opened this door, counselor. Let us let her speak her mind," said Mr. Justice Whitfield. "She's a woman, sir, women have resources of intuition denied you and me. Besides, there is a devil in all of us. Perhaps she recognized his devil."

Alison went on: "His manner, his voice, even his eyes were so unlike the Charles Collier I knew it was almost as if he was another person entirely. I'm not excusing his conduct, there's no excusing this terrible crime. I only know what I experienced, what I saw, what I felt, and I say that through desperation, or fear or cowardice, whatever the cause Charles behaved contrary to his nature, his real nature. He happens to be one of the finest men I have ever known and no matter what he did, no matter what he's guilty of it cannot erase his previous life. You can ask me questions till you're blue in the face, you'll never get me to turn against him!"

Silence, and then a curious interruption, the unmistakable sound of sobbing, a mournful and desperately lonely crying from the heart. All eyes turned to Charles Collier, shackled and seated, bent over, his hands covering his face, his shoulders shuddering with the wrenching grief that had seized him. He cried and cried while the gathering watched in hushed silence.

12

Mr. Justice Whitfield thanked Alison for her testimony and dismissed her from further participation in the trial. The clock in the Baptist Church steeple on the corner directly opposite the courthouse tolled twelve noon as she emerged from the building, made her way through the mob and, crossing the street, walked the two blocks down it to the bank where she had deposited her money earlier.

With Henry Porier's help, she got her thousand dollars back in cash and stuffing the money in her bag went at once to the livery stable and hired a horse and buggy.

Driving out to the Gilyards' farm, she turned over the events of the morning in her mind. There was little consolation to be gained from her defiance of the County Attorney beyond the fact that, if nothing else, Charles now knew that she had forgiven him. Why she had been so scrupulously specific in her written statement in recalling their conversations she would never know, but that was over with now.

Halfway to the farm, the sun emerged from behind a cloud and with its appearance the mood of sadness which had gripped her all morning long went away.

Turning in at the gate, she saw Braden Gilyard coming out of the barn. He waved and half ran up to the buggy, taking hold of her reins and helping her down.

"Alison! Alison!"

"Hagar in the wilderness," she said smiling. "How are you, Braden?"

"Just fine."

"And Jen?"

"The same. Come, let's go in."

Seeing their unexpected guest arrive through the front window, Mrs. Gilyard came out to meet them. Both remarked on how well she looked and asked all sorts of questions about the trial. They sat at the homemade table and had lunch, then while Mrs. Gilyard cleaned up the dishes, Alison and Braden moved into the front room to sit for a while and talk further.

He walked in front of her as they left the table and Mrs. Gilyard had already disappeared into the kitchen. Behind his back, Alison took the bundle of bills given her by Henry Porier out of her muff and slipped them into an empty vase on the whatnot shelf alongside the table.

It was only right, she had decided. She hadn't discussed it with Gene nor would she tell her mother when she got home. It was her money, her decision. The Gilyards had refused Maartens' offer of an equal amount; they needed money desperately and to her way of thinking they were entitled to every penny. Mrs. Gilyard probably wouldn't discover it in the vase for a day or so, long after she herself had returned to Philadelphia. Neither of the Gilyards had any idea where she came from and even if Mrs. Gilyard was able to recall Gene's name and her husband tracked him down at the hospital, she would see to it that Gene told him a white lie, that Hagar was from New York, from anyplace other than Philadelphia. It was the only way to get the money into their hands. They were far too proud to accept it handed over to them. A check in the post would be returned to the sender. Hiding it in the vase and dropping out of their lives, there was no possible way they could return it.

She went on her way, driving to Harwich and the hospital to meet Gene. Together they tried to visit Charles in his cell, but he refused to see either of them and the next morning she left for home.

Two weeks later she came upon an item on the front page of the Philadelphia newspaper:

BARRINGER HOUSE TRIAL
VERDICT GUILTY!

Brunswick, Me., Nov. 28. All three defendants in the notorious Barringer House Conspiracy trial have been found guilty, it was announced today by the County Attorney's office. Sentenced before Mr. Justice Whitfield were Herman Walter Mueller, a local funeral director who received life; Constance Marie Raphael, 20 years to life, and Dr. Charles Collier, life.

Mueller and Collier were remanded to the custody of the sheriff to be removed to State Prison in Taylorville. Raphael will serve her sentence in the Woman's Prison in Orono.

Dr. Hendrik Maartens alias Louis Hoorn alias Theo Vanderweg, mastermind of the bizarre conspiracy which succeeded in duping a number of individuals out of nearly $80,000 in the Brunswick area, was earlier removed to Albany, New York, to be tried on a separate charge of murder. Maartens' trial is in progress.

A week went by during which Alison spent interminably long hours discussing the case with her mother. She continued to search her mind and her conscience for something she might have overlooked which could have helped

Charles, but as time went on she came around to the view that everything possible had been done, that his trial had been a fair one and that, under the law, imprisonment was the only outcome possible.

A packet of news clippings arrived from Gene just before Christmas. Read in chronological order, they related the entire story of the trial and the results. One item in particular attracted her attention:

PHYSICIAN TO HANG FOR MURDER

> Albany, Dec. 16. Dr. Louis Hoorn, accused in the murder of Eleanor Lyons, was found guilty today in Bays Street Court and sentenced by Judge Justin T. Creel to be hanged.
>
> Dr. Hoorn's attorney, Samuel Watson, announced immediately the verdict was read that he will file an appeal in behalf of his client.

The Christmas season arrived and at Mrs. Collier's invitation Gene came down from Brunswick to share the holidays with them. Alison met him at the station and was surprised to see his face cloud when she caught his eye and waved.

The sights and sounds of Christmas were all around them, people laughing and singing, the bells of Christ Church ringing out melodiously and huge snowflakes falling like feathers as their carriage headed for Sedgley Avenue.

"What a terrible, terrible thing!" exclaimed Alison when he had finished explaining the reason for his cheerless expression.

"Evidently, Charles and this other fellow got into a loud

argument in the prison yard. The man had a knife, attacked Charles, stabbing him repeatedly. By the time the guards were able to break them apart and get poor Charles to the infirmary, he'd lost so much blood there wasn't a chance in the world of saving his life."

"What were they fighting about?"

"Henry Porier's uncle is captain of the guard over at Taylorville and he told Henry that it all started over money. Apparently Charles had accused the other fellow of stealing fifteen cents from him."

"Fifteen cents!"

"Yes. One more twisted link in the chain, I'm afraid."

"The last link."

"I went over to visit him three different times, but he refused to see me." Gene sighed and shook his head. "You know, darling, this marvelous city of yours has to be just as lovely in winter as it was in the fall. Here the snow mantles, in Brunswick it buries us."

In April of the following year Gene left his job at East Cumberland County Hospital and took a similar position on the administrative staff of Maas-Parkinson Hospital in Philadelphia. On the sixteenth of the month, the banns having been posted, he and Alison were married in Christ Church, Dr. Logan of Towlton School giving the bride away, Mrs. Collier directing the reception with the pride, confidence and efficiency of a general commanding his troops and Lydia weeping uncontrollably from the first notes of the organ to the last handful of rice tossed at the carriage carrying Mr. and Mrs. Eugene Hampton away on their honeymoon.

Two years later, on the fourteenth of March, 1854, in Maas-Parkinson Hospital, Mrs. Eugene Hampton gave birth to a baby at precisely three forty-one in the morning, much to the joy and relief of Mr. Eugene Hampton who had been pacing the floor in nervous anticipation since very early the previous evening. The little boy was the image of his father, red hair, blue eyes and, as the nurse in attendance observed, a perfectly adorable smile.

He was named Charles.